Jenna -
Thank you for
the Beautiful
Pictures !

Original COMING ATTRACTIONS Video store sign

Little Compton, Rhode Island

1983-1998

1

Cover Art and Illustrations by

Avery Feloni

www.averyfeloni.com

Dedicated to John Wilden Hughes

A filmmaker and storyteller who shaped a generation.

See how many movie lines you can guess.

(Answers in the back)

SOMERSET, MASSACHUSETTS

****

Somerset is a typical, quiet New England town. It has a church, a Diner, a few pizza places, a Cumberland Farms convenience store, and like most towns across America in 2004 there is a thriving video rental store. Tucked away at the far end of Main Street, just before the road becomes more residential, is the Wilden home, a small wood-shingled Cape-style house that doubles as the neighborhood video store and indelible fixture of Somerset weekend outings. Stenciled across the large bay window is a sign that reads: COMING ATTRACTIONS.

The inside of the Wilden house resembles a Blockbuster stockroom. Stacks of VHS tapes, Beta boxes, and DVD movie cases are piled high throughout every room.

Six-year-old Andrew Wilden sits at the kitchen table eating breakfast and staring at a movie playing on TV. His father James bounces into the room, a ball of frenetic energy. In his white smock and bow tie he looks more like a mad scientist than your friendly neighborhood video rental store owner.

Ding! The bell of an egg timer goes off.

"'*Get her. She's givin' out wings,*'" shouts Mr. Wilden with a cheery tone.

"IT'S A WONDERFUL LIFE!" replies young Andrew from the table.

"Very good, son," says Mr. Wilden patting his son on the head. "Wasn't that good, honey?"

His wife Allison Wilden doesn't answer. She stands by the sink, slowly turning eggs in a bowl, staring out the window with a tightly coiled sense of discontent and sadness in her eyes.

"'*In case I don't see ya, good afternoon, good evening, and good night!*'" James Wilden says kissing his wife on the cheek. She doesn't react. At all.

"Jim Carey. THE TRUMAN SHOW," shouts young Andrew from the table.

"That's my boy," replies the proud father.

"Gimme another one, Dad," Andrew asks. Mr. Wilden scrunches his face and looks at his son with a raised brow.

"Ok, um...'*Don't mess with the bull, young man. You'll get the horns.*'"

"Awe, that's an easy one," Andrew replies. "THE BREAKFAST CLUB.'

"Bing!" shouts gleeful Mr. Wilden.

"And that's Ned Ryerson from GROUNDHOG DAY," Andrew tells him.

"You're getting too good at this game," Mr. Wilden says with a wink. He grabs a bite of Andrew's toast and rushes off to open the store for the day.

Andrew continues to eat his breakfast. His eyes never leave the television.

Allison's eyes never leave the window.

****

Bells jingle above the COMING ATTRACTIONS entrance as customers hurry into the bustling store. VHS tapes and plastic DVD cases line the shelves. Movie posters cover the walls. A six-foot-tall cardboard cut-out of Spiderman stands beside Arnold Schwarzenegger's Terminator. James Wilden is truly in his element, happily ringing up orders and offering suggestions and cinematic advice to eager customers preparing for their weekends.

Andrew meanders through the aisles, his fingers brushing past each movie title. Romantic Comedy. Drama. Action. Adventure. Sci-Fi. Everything he would ever want to see is right here at his fingertips, all inside a small wood-shingled home in Somerset.

The laugher of children is heard from the sidewalk outside. Andrew rushes to the window to watch as kids happily walk past the store on their way home from school.

Allison Wilden bends beside her young son and whispers something in his ear. Andrew just nods and continues to peer through the window.

At its peak, Blockbuster video had over 9,000 stores worldwide and employed close to 85,000 people. Video rental outlets studded every city block and suburban strip mall across America. In 1989, a Blockbuster video store opened every 17 hours. But by 2014, it seemed as though the stores were closing at that same pace.

James Wilden, now 41, stands in his empty store. Time has done a number on him - he looks as confused and out of date as the tapes and DVD movies in his window display. The bells above the door jingle signaling that someone has entered the quiet store.

"Well hello, Michele," says Mr. Wilden, doing his best to be cheerful. "Haven't seen you here in a while."

"Hi, Mr. Wilden. Yeah, I've been away at school," replies Michele, looking a bit tired and hungover in her black and grey Providence College sweatshirt.

"College? My goodness, where has the time gone? Why, just yesterday you were a little girl renting all my Disney Princess movies."

"I know, right?" Michele replies with a reminiscent smile. She plops a plastic bag onto the counter and removes an assortment of VHS cassettes. "We were cleaning out my room and found these. Sorry. How much do I owe you?"

"Did you enjoy them?" asks Mr. Wilden.

"Sure. I guess."

"Maybe there was a line or two that made you smile? Made you think? Brought you to some kind of emotion? Movies can do that, you know. That's my payment," he tells her with all sincerity, then turns to the shelf behind him. "Now, if you liked this, let me show you another one of his films. Lots of romance and some of the wittiest dialogue you could ever..."

But Michele is already headed for the exit. "No, thank you, Mr. Wilden. I'll ...I'll just get it on Netflix or something."

And she's gone.

James Wilden walks to the window and watches as people walk past, heads down on their cell phones. No one notices his store - or the sadness and paranoia on his face.

*****

James Wilden stands beside a tall AV cart, the metal shelf just below the TV has an assortment of VHS cassette tapes. Classic '80's movies like THE BREAKFAST CLUB, SIXTEEN CANDLES, FERRIS BEULLER'S DAY OFF. He addresses his 'pupil' with a long wooden pointer in one hand and a black remote control in the other.

"Alright class, settle in. Now, let's see what we have today. Ooh, History," says Mr. Wilden as he grabs a VHS tape from the metal shelf and reads the sleeve. "THE HISTORY OF THE WORLD - Mel Brooks' comic genius is unleashed in spades in this episodic spoof of history's seminal moments."

The lone pupil, Andrew Wilden, has grown into a handsome sixteen-year-old teenager with a mop of wavy hair and sleepy, brown eyes. He timidly speaks up. "You know, Dad, I was thinking - maybe it's time I take classes at the High School."

Mr. Wilden is busy loading the cassette into the VCR. He spins to address the 'class.' "School? Why? We've covered all the basic curriculum. Biology. Science. Math."

"We watched GOOD WILL HUNTING," Andrew says flatly.

"Yes," replies Mr. Wilden, reciting from memory. "A troubled genius must come to grips with his childhood demons in order to embrace the possibilities his intellect can provide."

"That's not really teaching me math, Dad," replies Andrew, knowing he has to tread lightly. "Like, for Biology we watched HAPPY FEET."

Mr. Wilden recites. "Ah, yes. The fascinating story of an Antarctic colony whose rituals of mating..."

Andrew doesn't let his father finish. "It's about singing, dancing penguins," he says flatly.

"Yes, but they are *Emperor* penguins, Andrew," he tells him, then turns his attention back to the VCR. "I'm sure there was some biology in there."

Andrew takes a deep breath, knowing this next part isn't going to be well received. "Yeah, but...I'm not sure how all this is gonna look on my college applications."

Mr. Wilden stops what he's doing and turns to face his son. "College? Don't be silly, you need to help me and your mother with the store."

Andrew softens his delivery. "Dad, I...I don't think Mom's coming back."

The words sit there for a moment as Mr. Wilden's face shows his confusion.

"She'll be back. You'll see. Nobody leaves a movie halfway through. You want to see how it ends, right?" replies Mr. Wilden walking to the window. He looks up and down the street with an eerie sort of paranoia. "Those people just went to work. Kids just went to school. No, son. We'll stay right here."

CLICK. The television screen flickers to life as the movie/class begins. Mr. Wilden leans back with a sense of comfort and resolve. "See Andrew, everything you need is in the movies."

The glow of the television bounces off Andrew's concerned face as he is starting to realize how odd and confused his father has become.

****

Andrew stands at the kitchen sink slowly turning eggs in a bowl with the same sense of sadness and discontent his mother showed years ago. When Allison Wilden left, Andrew took over the responsibilities of keeping the house. No note. No goodbye. No explanation. Andrew just woke up one morning, turned on the TV (like always) and waited for his mother to come into the kitchen and start breakfast. That was three years ago. Once he saw that her clothes were packed and gone too, Andrew knew it was permanent - something his father refuses to believe or even acknowledge.

Andrew's eyes look to the window, roaming the world outside – the world his mother now lives in. Maybe she will be back, like his father believes. Maybe.

He shakes the thoughts and begins to bark out movie lines. "'*Okay, campers, rise and shine, and don't forget your booties 'cause it's cooooold out there today. It's cooool out there every day'.*"

POOF! A gas burner lights the stove.

"'*You come on down here and chum some of this shhhhh...'*" he shouts, sizzling eggs on a hot pan.

"'Saddle up. We're burning daylight!'"

The house is silent. Andrew heads upstairs to rouse his father.

"'Come on, Dad. Dad. Dad. Dad, Dad, Dad.'"

Nothing. A bedroom door swings open. Andrew enters the room. "Time to get up, Dad. Dad? Dad!!"

James Wilden sits huddled in a corner, gently rocking back and forth, a blank look of terror on his face.

CHARLTON MEMORIAL HOSPITAL

****

Danny Muldoon, a handsome, eager-to-please, cop with a kind babyface that makes him look younger than his thirty-six years, is huddled in the corner with his Somerset Police partner Frank Kobolowski, a twenty-five-year veteran of the Somerset police force with a paunch gut and white-walled military-style 'Boys Regular' haircut. It's the exact same haircut he's had since he sat in the swivel leather chair at Jimmy DeVito's Barber Shop when he was seven. Frank Kobolowski isn't just Old School —

he's brick-and-mortar-you-can-keep-all-your-flashy-shiny-new-stuff Old School.

Muldoon reaches into the breast pocket of his uniform for his trusty, never without it, palm-sized notepad. "No known relatives. Neighbors say the mother left a few years back."

"You get an address at least?" asks Kobolowski, tugging at the belt of his expanding gut.

Muldoon refers to the notepad. "They lived upstairs from the video store off Main."

"COMING ATTRACTIONS? That place is still open?" states Kobolowski. "Jesus, I think I still got a copy of TOP GUN from there. Late fees are gonna be a bitch."

Of course he rented TOP GUN, Muldoon thinks to himself. It's a movie with just the right amount of macho, reflector sunglasses, and military whitewall haircuts that Kobolowski loves. Muldoon approaches Andrew in the waiting room and reads from his trusty notepad.

"Alright, ah, young man. You are…" He consults the notepad. "Andrew Wilden. Is that correct?"

Silence. Muldoon goes back to the notes.

"We have one male. Caucasian. Forty-one years of age. And a reported 10-57."

Kobolowski rolls his eyes and steps in to help. "That's a missing person, son. Sorry, Officer Muldoon here isn't really good at talking. Your mom. Do you know where she is? Son? No?"

Andrew sits there in silence. Kobolowski pulls Muldoon aside.

"You got a great way with people there, Dan," he says, then reaches into his pocket for a business card. "Here. You're gonna need to call this place."

Muldoon's face turns flush with panic. He recognizes the name on the card.

"Can't...can't you call?" he pleads.

"All you, big guy. Just be your charming, chatty self," says Kobolowski full of attitude.

PETERSON HOUSE

****

The Peterson house is a large Victorian in varying degrees of mess. Bowls sit in the sink. Papers are strewn on tables. Piles of books lay on the floor. Three dogs bark and scramble enthusiastically to greet Claire Peterson as she enters the kitchen, half a bagel in her mouth, hopping on one leg trying to get on a shoe. She is running late – again.

"I gotta run," Claire speaks to someone in the other room. "Sorry about last night. I was tired and cranky and, well, sometimes a girl just wants to come home and slip into a bath of wine, ya know?"

Silence.

"That was a joke. Sort of. Ok, so, I gotta go. I'll see you later. There's milk in the fridge, try and make yourself something to eat."

More silence.

"This is good, right? Right?" she says, then hops out the door - shoe in hand, bagel in mouth.

SOMERSET HIGH SCHOOL

****

Kids shuffle through the halls past rows of lockers, earplugs in, heads down, texting on their latest iPhones and smart tablets. Flat screen TV monitors hang from the ceiling and scroll morning announcements, but no one is paying attention.

Three girls gather around a locker. They're pretty, popular, and Plastic - each one interchangeable with the next and so cookie cutter and similar - they dress alike, they talk alike, they act alike - that it's hard for anyone to tell them apart.

"Oh. My. Gawd," says Plastic 1. "Did you see what happened on REAL HOUSEWIVES last night?"

"Don't. I have it on DVR," replies Plastic 2, never once looking up from her phone. None of them do.

"Tell her what happened," urges Plastic 3.

"No! Nobody say a thing. Not a word," snaps Plastic 2.

Plastic 1 finally looks up from her phone long enough to see Molly Peterson standing at the locker behind her. Molly wears glasses, has straight hair with wispy bangs and wears bland clothing. She is so plain that she stands out among this flashy trio, and so fiercely independent that she doesn't care.

"Don't look at me," Molly tells them. "I've never seen it."

"Seriously?" asks Plastic 2.

"We don't have a television," states Molly with a matter of fact air of confidence. She's come to accept her television-less situation. In fact, she's even kind of proud of it in today's 'Must See TV' society.

 The "we don't have a television" remark causes all three Plastics look up from their phones in shock.

"So, like, you've seen nothing?" asks Plastic 3. "No AMERICAN IDOL? Or VANDERPUMP RULES?

Molly closes her locker with aplomb. "Nope."

"Seriously? Wait. So, like, not even THE KARDASHIANS?!" asks Plastic 1 totally bewildered.

"Sadly, no," replies Molly dripping with sarcasm and loving it.

Plastic 1 returns to the important task at hand - typing on her phone what is certainly the most important message that has ever been written. (for the record it's a reply ROFL to an earlier LOL which was a response to a well-timed LMAO...you know, important stuff like that)

"Guys, you have to come over and watch THE BACHELOR tonight. It's the final rose." says Plastic 2.

"Definitely. I'll text Katie and Lindsey to come too," replies Plastic 3.

Suddenly, a voice yells, "Whadd-up ladies?" It's Michael Johnson - known around the halls of Somerset High as Skype. Skype is your typical doughy, zitty Freshman, constantly overcompensating his appearance and status by trying to act waaaay cooler than he is.

"You want to be in my SnapChat story?" he asks attempting to take a video with his cell phone. The Plastics look at him with disgust.

"I'm gonna be famous one day," he tells them. "You can say you knew me when."

A cell phone buzzes. Skype looks to the girls as he answers it with an air of cocky confidence. "Probably one of my crew. My boys are always hittin' me up," he says placing the phone to his ear. "Whadd-up playah?"

A woman's voice is heard.

"Michael, you left your Romeo and Juliet book at home. I found it in your room. And why, young man, is your underwear still not picked up? I'm not touching it!"

Oh God. It's Skype's mother Mrs. Johnson on speaker. What a nightmare! He fumbles to find the mute button, the volume button, *any* button.

"You want me to drive it to school for you, sweetie? Michael? Hello?" she says for everyone to hear.

The three Plastics walk away laughing as Skype slumps against the locker and tries to recover from the damage. Finally locating the speaker button, he speaks into the phone. "It's OK, Mom. I don't...Yeah. Yup. Love you too. Bye."

He turns to Molly. "Hey."

"Hey, Skype...Sorry, I mean Michael," she corrects herself.

"That's cool, I'm used to it. My crew calls me Skype now, so..." he stops, knowing this act is lost on Molly. She could care less about Cool and Status and Wanna-Be's. "Can I borrow your Shakespeare notes?" he asks. "I really don't need my mother walking the halls calling out my name."

Molly smiles. "Sure, but you'll need to write your own essay. Form your own opinion and ideas. That's the only way you're going to create original thought."

Skype smirks with confidence. "I'm saving all my 'original' thoughts to become an internet sensation. YouTube. Snapchat. Vine. Do you know some dude made five million dollars last year posting videos?"

"I wouldn't know," says Molly. "My mom literally just let me get Facebook."

Skype does his best to act chill. "Yeah? You, ah...you can friend me if you want."

"Sure," she replies." I'll do it later."

"Promise?!" says Skype a little more enthusiastically than he intended.

"Of course," replies Molly with a sincere smile closing the locker and handing over her Shakespeare notes. "You'll be my one and only Facebook friend."

Skype watches her walk away and mutters sadly, "Yeah. Mine too."

DEPARTMENT OF CHILD PROTECTIVE SERVICES

****

Claire Peterson's tiny office mirrors the disheveled mess at home. Bulging manila folders and papers are stacked and laid out everywhere. Half-full, days old cups of Starbucks coffee are strewn about. She rummages through the desk and hears a feint tap at the door.

"On a bit of a search and rescue mission here. What's up?" she yells out from behind the mess.

Officer Muldoon stands in the doorway, terrified. He's worse at talking with women than he is with teenagers. "Sorry to interrupt, Ma'am. We, uh, we have a 10-57. That's a missing person, Ma'am. One…"

He reaches for his ever-present, trusty notepad. "Allison Wilden. There's an ATL…"

"ATL?" asks Claire never looking up.

"Attempt-to-locate, Ma'am. We also have a Caucasian male. Forty-one. A Mister James Wilden. Infirmed. Leaving one…"

Back to the notepad.

"Andrew John Wilden. Sixteen. Also, Caucasian. Also, male. He's to be remanded to the state until such time as parental support can be re-established and..."

Claire finally stops her search and rescue mission to look up. "Stop," she says. "Is that him out there? What's his name? Andrew, you said?"

"Yes, Ma'am. Andrew. His father, is infirmed for an undetermined period..."

"In English please, officer," Claire tells him. Muldoon adjusts his tone and nervously delivers the news.

"His dad is in the hospital - some sort of breakdown. They're not sure how long he'll be there, and, well, we can't find his mother. He has no one...Ma'am."

A softness falls on Claire's face. She looks to the sad, lonely boy sitting outside her office.

"Has he been sitting out there long?"

"No, Ma'am. Well, yes, Ma'am. We arrived at 0900. Apparently, you were running late," Muldoon tells her.

"Yeah. I get that a lot," murmurs Claire.

"Well, unfortunately, there's no local Foster Care available right now. We may have to send him to Fall River."

Muldoon is a bit taken back. Fall River is not a great option - it's a tougher population of teenager with a high crime rate, the kind of place that a quiet kid like Andrew could easily get lost in the cracks.

"There's nothing here at all?" Muldoon asks, genuinely feeling bad. Claire senses his emotion and finally looks up at Muldoon for the first time. 'Hmm. He's kinda cute,' she thinks to herself, then her wheels start spinning.

"What did you say your name was Officer?" Claire asks nicely.

"Muldoon, Ma'am. Daniel Muldoon. Actually, we, ah, we went to High..."

"You married Officer Muldoon? Kids?" Claire cuts him off.

"Me? No, Ma'am," says Muldoon turning bright red. "I used to reside, I mean, lived with my mother, but she recently..."

Claire sees her opportunity and jumps at the opening. "So, you have plenty of room. Great, he could stay with you."

Muldoon stumbles. "Me? Oh, no Ma'am. I'm not very good with…"

Claire isn't listening. She's already heads down filling out the application. "I'll start paperwork for emergency housing."

"Wait, what?" asks Muldoon.

"Small town, small rules. It's only a temporary court order until we find more local Foster Care, or you figure out this 10-54 business."

"10-54 is livestock on the highway, Ma'am," Muldoon replies automatically.

"Well, be thankful I'm not asking you to live with a cow," Claire replies with a smirk. "That was a joke. This is good, right? Right?"

"Yes, Ma'am. I mean no, Ma'am. Wait, what?"

"Officer Muldoon?"

"Ma'am?"

"Bring Andrew in. I'd like to say hello," Claire instructs him.

"Yes, Ma'am." Totally bamboozled, he escorts Andrew in.

"Andrew, this is Miss Peterson," Muldoon says, then bends closer, talks louder. "I-said-this-is-Miss-Peterson."

Claire rolls her eyes. "Danny?" she says with a soft tone.

Muldoon eagerly looks up. "Yes, Ma'am?"

"Go. You two will have plenty of time to get to know each other."

Muldoon's shoulder slump. He stumbles away with a sort of 'what the heck just happened' kind of look as Claire goes back to search mode and rifles through the desk.

"You wanna tell me what school you're from?" she asks.

Andrew is silent.

"No? Not very chatty, huh? That's OK, I'm sort of used to that. We'll need to get you settled in. Somerset High School, home of the Red Raiders. Although, my mother says you're not supposed to call them that. It's insensitive to Indians or something - the feather kind not the dot kind. Aha! Found it."

Claire sits up, her mouth full of bagel, and victoriously yells, "Go Raiders! Yeah!"

SOMERSET HIGH SCHOOL

****

Andrew anxiously walks the halls beside Claire, his eyes taking it all in. Everything is so new and colorful and wondrous and loud – or at least it seems that way to Andrew Wilden. Fresh paint on the walls. Carpet in the library.

The bell rings and chaos begins. Doors open, releasing students, surging like salmon into the hall. Claire and Andrew meander their way through the maze and cacophony of students.

"Wait here. I'll find out where you're supposed to be," Claire shouts above the noise.

Andrew leans against a locker, trying not to be noticed. Kids hurry past, heads down on their cell phones, ignoring him, ignoring each other. A few glance in his direction, but there's no sign of friendship in their faces - they are all too busy texting, checking their Instagram posts, Facebook likes, and Snapchat stories.

And that's when we meet Ricky Sherman and his ever-present posse of Sidekicks making their way through the school.

"Outta the way, losers," barks overgrown jock Ricky as he pushes weaker nerdy kids.

"Yeah. Outta the way, losers," repeats one of the Sidekicks. They pretty much repeat everything Ricky says, only louder, and then high-five every time Ricky does something super cool and awesome.

Andrew's eyes squint. He's seen the bully Ricky Sherman character in every teenage High School movie. Biff Tannen. Scut Farkus. Johnny Lawrence. Fred O'Bannion. They're all the same. Blustery blowhards who act like Kings of the school, strutting around like they are the cool guys, the bad asses, the ones everyone wants to be - or at least that's what they think.

"Ah, what are you doing?" asks Ricky eyeing Andrew up and down. "You're standing in front of my locker. Move!"

"You heard him!" repeats a Sidekick right on cue. "Move!"

Andrew stays silent and stands motionless.

"Who is this kid?" Ricky asks with a quizzical stare. The bell rings signaling the need to hurry off to class - but not before Ricky throws a fake punch in Andrew's direction.

But Andrew doesn't flinch. Not at all.

Claire is running late, as always, and hurries down the hall. "Making friends already?" she says breathlessly doing her best to help sell the situation. "Good for you. So, hmmm, Vernon Gleason. I can't believe he's still teaching here. Well, yay for High School. This is good, right? Right?"

****

Every school has one teacher like Vernon Gleason. He's your typical 'asshole-power-hungry-know-it-all- who- hates-his-life-but -hates-the-kids-even-more' kinda guy. The students have yet to figure out if his permanently red face is the result of bad psoriasis, flush rosacea, or high blood pressure. Most say it's a combination of all three, mostly attributed to the lack of patience he has for his students.

Claire enters the classroom with Andrew in tow and plops a manila folder onto Mr. Gleason's desk.

"Mr. Gleason, this is Andrew Wilden," she tells him. "He's a recent transfer to the district."

"Wonderful," snaps Mr. Gleason with an exaggerated, blustery eye roll. "More minds, same pay rate. Two hundred and sixty-three days left 'till retirement. Not counting snow days."

"Love the dedication there, Vern," quips Claire. She turns to Andrew and whispers, "he hasn't changed since I had him a hundred years ago."

Andrew finds a seat in the front, between Skype and Molly.

Claire points at Molly as she heads out the door. "Be careful of that one, Andrew. She's wicked smaht," she says with a sly wink and exaggerated Boston accent.

Molly slumps in her seat. She just wants to die.

"Home schooled, huh?" growls Mr. Gleason reviewing Andrew's folder. "Great. Another living room Einstein. Well, I'll try to be as *fascinating* as your last teacher. So glad I got my Doctorate in Education."

Ricky fakes a cough and yells, "Loser." The whole class giggles. Andrew hates it here already.

"Mister Sherman," snaps Gleason. "Why don't you enlighten us with the homework assignment from last evening."

Ricky sits up with a look of sheer panic and glares directly at Skype. "Don't you, like, have it on your desk, Mr. Gleason?" he asks.

"No, Mister Sherman, I, *like,* don't. Am I, *like,* supposed to?" replies Gleason mocking him.

"I...I..." stammers Ricky.

"I is for idiot," barks Gleason. "Is that what you think I am, Mister Sherman? An idiot? I've seen this movie before son - and it doesn't end well. It's very simple, actually. I teach. You learn. Get a diploma. Get a job. Pay taxes. Fund my retirement. See? Simple."

Mr. Gleason turns toward the chalkboard and mumbles, "Why do I even get out of bed for you people."

Suddenly, a voice from behind says, *"Eat. My. Shorts."*

Gleason spins to face the class. "What? Who said that? Who said that!"

No one moves a muscle. Gleason looks homicidal. The bright red psoriasis/rosacea/blood pressure is off the charts. "Maybe getting an extra chapter to review tonight will help somebody speak up," he snarls.

The class groans.

Skype and Molly look curiously at Andrew. He just sits between them in silence, staring straight ahead.

PETERSON HOUSE

****

Claire drops an armful of folders onto the already cluttered front entranceway. She kicks off her shoes and calls out to someone in the next room.

"I hope you made yourself something to eat. Yes? No? Well, that must be how you keep such a svelte manly figure, huh?"

Nothing.

"Met a new kid today," Claire continues as she sorts through the mail. "Interesting case. His father is in the hospital and they can't find his mother. He must have one. I mean, even you have a mother, right? Right?"

Still nothing.

"Sweet kid as far as I can tell. He doesn't talk much. He's the strong silent type," she says making her way to the next room. "And you know how I'm a sucker for the quiet ones."

Claire stands in the doorway and looks at her son, ten-year-old Benjamin, sitting quietly at a table assembling Legos with swift progression and determination. He rocks gently back and forth, self-stimming, without affect or eye contact. She leans in to kiss her son on the forehead, but Ben jerks away, emotionless. She can never get used to that.

****

Nana May Peterson, a Flower Power aging hippie that reeks of patchouli oils and incense, sits meditating on the living room floor surrounded by candles. The trio of barking dogs break her trance when they rush to greet Claire.

"Ugh. It's like a Goddamn PETCO in here," snaps Nana May. "Sit. Sit! These dogs never listen to me."

"Awe be nice to my babies," says Claire crouching to pet her beloved dogs. "Sorry I was running late this morning."

"You're always running late, my dear. You need to find balance," her earthy-crunchy mother tells her.

"Can't just Zen my way through life, Ma."

"It works for me," replies Nana May sincerely meaning it as she rolls up her yoga mat and blows out the candles.

"Did Ben leave his room at all today?" Claire asks.

"Not really. You know, maybe we could try another school," says Nana May treading lightly. She knows this is a touchy subject.

41

"We've been over this, Mom," snaps Claire. Yep. It's a *real* touchy subject.

"I know, Hon, but there are a lot of other places. I've read about one school that..."

But Claire doesn't let her finish. "Mom. I'm not...I mean, Ben's not ready." She stops herself, realizing that it came out wrong.

"Sorry. I'm sure if I just close my eyes and breathe through my nose, everything will be fine," Claire recites, breathlessly mocking her mother.

Nana May cups her daughter's face with her hand and recites, *"Oh Michael from mountains. Go where you will go to. Know that I will know you. Someday I may know you very well."*

"That from one of your meditation gurus?" Claire asks.

"Yup," replies her mother with a soft smile. "Joni Mitchell."

The dogs scramble and bark as the back door opens and Molly walks in with a backpack over her shoulder.

"There's my girl. Mwah!" says Nana May greeting her granddaughter with a kiss. She holds up a Peace sign and floats out the door. "Gotta run, kids. Final rose on The Bachelor tonight."

Molly drops her backpack among the books piled on the living room floor. "I can't believe how you embarrassed me in school today Mom!"

"Please. That's part of a mother's job description," Claire tells her. "Did you happen to see mine just float out the back door?"

"Even my Grandmother is cooler than I am. Are we ever gonna get a TV in this house?" Molly asks.

"You know the reason."

"I know. But it's embarrassing."

Claire cups her daughter's face with her hand, just like her own mother did, and begins to recite, *"I invite you to sit down in front of your television. I can assure you that you will observe a..."*

"...vast wasteland," says Molly finishing the sentence and pulling away. "I know, Mom. You use that quote all the time. Gawd, is there anyone with an original thought anymore? I just want to know that someone understands. I need to know these people exist."

"I'm sure they do, sweetie," Claire reassures her daughter. "So, how did Andrew make out today?"

"Who?"

"The new kid in Mr. Gleason's class."

"He seems kinda bizarre," says Molly.

"Well, I think he needs a friend. You should invite him over."

"And do what?" snaps the ever-emotional teenager. "Ooh, I know. Maybe we could watch the fish tank and make believe we're watching an underwater sea adventure."

"Don't be like that," Claire scolds.

Molly mockingly cups her mother's face with her hand and begins to recite; *"When television is good, nothing - not the theater, not magazines or newspapers - nothing is better."*

"Who says so?" asks Claire.

"Newton Minow. In that same speech," her smart-as-a-whip daughter schools her.

"Well, I don't remember that part," replies Claire knowing Molly is right. "Now go say hello to your brother, smarty pants."

Claire can't help but smile a little, then - "Aaargh!" she screams stepping on a razor-sharp plastic Lego. "And tell him to come pick these things up!"

MULDOON'S APARTMENT

****

Andrew stands in a dim, cramped living room with a duffle bag of clothes hanging over his shoulder.   Officer Muldoon begins the tour.

"So, um, let's see. Kitchen is over there. Living room. Bathroom to the left. Roger that. Any questions so far?"

Nothing. Just awkward, painful silence. This is going to be tough.

"Just temporary," Muldoon mutters to himself. "It will be good, she said. Right? Right?"

The flick of a lamp illuminates a bedroom that appears to belong to an old woman – or at least it used to. A crucifix hangs on a bare wall. A knitted afghan blanket is folded neatly on the edge of the tightly made bed. Muldoon stares for a moment, then breaks the silence.

"This is...well, this used to be my mother's room. She, um, she passed away a little while ago." Andrew makes eye contact for the first time. It's a connection, a small one, a momentary recognition of the loss of mothers.

"I usually fall asleep with the television on," says Muldoon trying to fill the awkward silence. "My mother used to listen to Jay Leno every night. I was more of a Letterman guy. Now, I don't even know who the Late Night hosts are anymore." He looks back at the TV in the living room with sadness. "I just... I like to leave the TV on, if that's OK."

Andrew is fine with that. In fact, it may be the one thing that reminds him of home.

"Well, I'll, ah, I'll let you get settled in," says Muldoon as he quietly leaves.

Andrew sits alone on the edge of the bed. He reaches into his pocket and removes a small black television remote control. It's the one that used to belong to his father. He lays back and stares up at the slow rotating ceiling fan above his head, clutching the black remote closely to his chest.

SOMERSET HIGH SCHOOL

★★★★

Andrew's first day in a real school. Everything is loud and fast and difficult and strange. Kids stream past, heads down, earplugs in, no one talking to each other. Everyone hates Mondays – it doesn't matter what age you are.

Andrew fumbles with the combination on his locker. How the hell do you work this thing? Skype move in to help when - WHACK! - he's slammed against the lockers. Yep. Ricky Sherman and the Sidekicks right on cue. Ricky grabs the cell phone from Skype's hand and holds it high out of reach.

"Filming people when they're not looking again, Perv?" snarls Ricky with a real bitterness in his voice.

"What? Naw, dude, no," says Skype trying his best to be cool. "It's just videos. Snapchats. YouTube. You know, stuff like that."

"Yeah?" snaps Ricky. "How come I never seen anything?"

"I...I haven't posted them yet," Skype admits with a sheepish tone.

"Yeah, well keep it that way, dickhead. Nobody wants to see your stupid loser videos," Ricky snarls. The Sidekicks laugh and high-five like the cartoon characters they are. "What happened to my homework yesterday?"

Using Molly's advice, Skype says, "My man, you really need to think for yourself. You know, form your own opinion and ideas. That's the only way you'll ever create original thought."

SLAM! His head meets the locker again.

"My man?!" growls Ricky. "You better hand that in to Gleason. Like, today!"

"Yeah, yeah, sure," replies Skype. "I just thought, well, Mr. Gleason pretty much knows my handwriting and..."

"That's the problem. Don't think. Just get it done. You got that...*Skype*?!" Ricky says spitting the word to punctuate his anger. He tosses the cell phone into the air and walks away. Skype watches helplessly as it twirls towards the ground.

Suddenly, a hand reaches out and snatches the phone just before impact. It's Andrew.

"Thanks," says Skype trying to recover and regain some sense of cool in front of the new kid. "Me and my boy Ricky - we're always foolin' around like that."

He attempts to high-five a passing student. "Yo, what up brother man?" The kid ignores him. Andrew turns back to his locker, spinning the combination and still struggling to get it open.

"Forget it," Skype tells him. "Someone probably jammed the door. Or glued the lock." He knows. That happens to his locker all the time.

"Name's Skype. Not sure I can squeeze another dude into my squad, but...Yo, dap it, my man."

Skype is left hanging again by another passing student. He shakes it off and begins to escort Andrew down the hall.

"We got it all here at Somerset High, so you're gonna wanna pick the right crew, you know?"

He begins to point out the different groups assembled in packs along the hallway. "Freaks. Geeks. Rainbows. Jocks. Hipsters."

Andrew's eyes scan the students. "'*The brain. The athlete. The basketcase. The princess. The criminal.*'"

50

Skype scrunches his face and asks, "BREAKFAST CLUB?"

"*Bing!*" Andrew replies and walks away.

Skype nods his head and smirks, "Ooh, I like that new kid."

PETERSON HOUSE

****

Claire hops on one leg, trying to get on a shoe, a half-eaten bagel hanging from her mouth. She's late, as always, and yells to the other room.

"Come on, Ben. I'm really late. Just tell me what you're looking for and I'll help you find it."

The negotiations begin.

"I'll buy you two if we can just leave now. Benjamin! We need to go to Nana May's!"

But Ben is having a complete meltdown, desperate to find what he's looking for.

"Just tell me what you want! Let me help you, Ben. Talk to me!" she pleads. Ben starts to kick and scream. Claire is frantically trying to help.

They're both a mess.

It's only 8:30 in the morning.

Everyone hates Mondays.

SOMERSET HIGH SCHOOL

****

A bell rings and, two by two, kids scramble to sit at Biology lab tables. Andrew attempts to find a seat and accidentally bumps into Molly. He shifts left. So does Molly. Then right. She does too. Their eyes hold a moment. It's awkward, but there's an unusual sort of spark between them. They brush it off and look to grab a seat.

Skype watches the exchange from his table and spots an opportunity. "Ah, I'm sorry, Miss Ludwig," he says standing up. "But I refuse to take part in this barbaric ritual. Frog populations are dwindling, and I couldn't live with the guilt."

"Sit down please, Michael," Miss Ludwig tells him.

But Skype is already collecting his things, leaving Molly alone at his table. "Besides, I'm a strict vegetarian, and, um, it's against my religion to eat meat. Or carve meat. Either way, I'm outta here."

"*Hasta la Vista, baby,'* he whispers to Andrew on the way out. "That's from a movie."

Yeah. Andrew knows.

Ricky Sherman enthusiastically raises his hand from the back of the Lab. "I'll partner up with Molly, Miss Ludwig."

Molly rolls her eyes. She has no patience for a lot of the kids in her grade, especially the Cookie-Cutter Plastics and the I'm-So-Cool-Look-at-Me Jocks - people who overuse the words 'awesome' and 'like' and try to make rules that her fiercely independent spirit refuses to obey. Molly just wants one person, *any* person, she can bond with. Someone beyond the, *like,* Plastics, and the, *like, awesome,* Jocks. Someone smart and funny and independent and original. Is that too much to ask?

Miss Ludwig looks at Andrew still struggling to find a Lab partner. "Andrew, why don't you come up here and take Michael's seat."

The chair squeals against the floor as Andrew pulls it out and sits in awkward silence beside Molly. Neither make eye contact. It was embarrassing enough when they almost head butted each other scrambling to get into the Lab, now they have to sit together? After what seems like an eternity, Molly speaks. "So, have you done this before?"

"Me?" asks Andrew timidly. "Ah, sure. But, it...it was with penguins."

"You dissected a penguin?!" exclaims Molly loudly – too loudly because the class laughs. She immediately feels bad.

"No. No. I mean, I studied biology before. Sort of," Andrew replies, his voice trailing off. He feels so stupid and out of place.

The smell of formaldehyde fills the room as Miss Ludwig opens jars and begins to distribute frogs to the class. A huge frog is dropped onto the tray in front of Molly and Andrew. This frog is enormous! It's literally overflowing out the sides.

Molly is a bit squeamish. "You wanna cut, Andrew? Andrew?"

Andrew stares off, speechless, then says, "'You're gonna need a bigger boat.'"

She looks at him, confused. "Huh?"

Andrew corrects himself. "Knife. I mean...you're...you're gonna need a bigger knife."

Molly gives a faint smile, thinking to herself, 'He's kinda funny. And cute.' Andrew feels relieved and a little more confident using a movie line.

Ricky sits in the back of the room watching their whole interaction – definitely not happy.

CHILD PROTECTIVE SERVICES

****

"Excuse me, Ma'am. I'm...I'm not interrupting, am I?" asks Officer Muldoon standing in the doorway with two coffees.

"Tough morning," sighs Claire, completely frazzled. "I had to find a missing dinosaur."

Muldoon gives her a confused look.

"My son. He was looking for his lost plastic dinosaur this morning. Is there a code for that? Like a 10-56 or something?" she asks.

"10-56 is an intoxicated pedestrian, Ma'am," replies Muldoon in his ever-present Cop-speak, clearly not getting the joke. After a beat, he realizes she's just kidding. "Now, if the dinosaur had been drinking, that could potentially be considered a 10-56 and, well, we'd have to respond."

Claire gives a faint smile, thinking to herself, 'He's kinda funny. And cute.'

"Is that coffee?" she asks.

"Yes, Ma'am. I didn't have the intel on how you take it, so I got everything."

He's not kidding. The cardboard tray in his hand is overflowing with sugars, Sweet-and-Low, half and half, skim milk, Lactaid, and flavored creams – it's literally everything the Diner offers that one would use with their coffee.

"Sit," Claire commands. He obeys – just like one of her dogs. "At least someone listened to me today. Master's in Psychology, and I can't get a ten-year-old out the door in the morning."

Claire sips her coffee like it is literally the best thing she has ever had in her life. She sits back and reflects. "I hated being late. Even by a minute. I used to be so organized."

"I remember," says Muldoon, letting his guard down. "You always had those colored pens and unicorn notebooks."

"Wait, what?" says Claire. Muldoon turns bright red. He is so busted.

"You went to Somerset High?"

"I…I was pretty quiet back then," Muldoon replies.

"I'm so sorry, Danny. I didn't remember," Claire admits, then gives a reminiscent little smile, more melancholy than sad. "God, that seems like a lifetime ago. Go Raiders, right? So, how's Andrew doing?"

"Good," Muldoon replies. "I mean, I guess. I don't know. He doesn't really talk much."

She nods and gives a look that says, 'I know the feeling.'

"That's the reason I'm here, Ma'am," Muldoon continues. "I wanted to talk to you about the living quarters situation. You see, I..."

But Claire isn't listening. She's lost in her coffee and memories of High School when life was calmer, slower, more organized. She snaps out of the trance and asks, "Any news on his mother?"

"No. No updates to report, Ma'am. We've made inquiries, but as of 0-900..."

Claire stops him. "Do you always talk like that?"

"Ma'am?"

"Like you're quoting from some police manual."

"No, Ma'am. Yes, Ma'am," Muldoon replies, embarrassed.

"Claire. It's just, Claire. OK? And Danny?" she asks.

"Yes, Ma'...I mean, yes, Claire."

"Next time - skim milk, no sugar. This is good, right? Right?"

Muldoon smiles. Yep, this is good.

****

The top three most common fears in the Unites States are:

1. Arachnophobia - fear of spiders.
2. Ophidiophobia - fear of snakes.
3. Acrophobia - fear of heights.

So far, no one has come up with a word for probably the most terrifying thing on earth - finding a seat in your High School cafeteria....as a Freshman...and a new kid.

Tables are set in order of popularity. The Plastics sit near the bathroom so they can quickly access the mirrors to do any last-minute beauty checks. The Jocks sit near the food, so they don't have to walk too far to get their third and fourth helpings of Sloppy Joe's and grilled chicken sandwiches. Freaks, the ones who typically wear black lipstick and black clothes and black everything, hang out by the door so they can smoke cigarettes and never smile. And all the Geeks and Nerds huddle in a corner at the back of the cafeteria closest to all the electrical outlets so they can stay fully charged playing video games on their laptops and tablets.

Andrew slowly makes his way through the intimidating cafeteria, tray in hand, looking for somewhere to sit. He spots Skype's backpack and jacket at an empty table next to the area designated for Nerds and Geeks. It's in the back - the way, *way* back. He slides into an empty chair and opens the laptop Skype left on the table. Looking around, he quickly types ALLISON WILDEN into the search bar. His eyes scan the results. Over fourteen million matches. Teachers. Doctors. Students. All shapes and sizes and backgrounds, all sharing the same name. None of them are his mother.

Suddenly Ricky Sherman slams the laptop shut. He plops beside Andrew and leans in menacingly close. "Let me explain a few ground rules for ya, kid. I go to class, I just don't *'go'* to class," he says using air quotes. "C's get degrees, brother. Understand? I need to pass to keep playing on Friday nights. You see, I got a system here - a pecking order if you will."

He points to the nearby pack of Geeks and Nerds. "They do the work for me, and I let them survive High School. Fair trade if you ask me."

Andrew listens intently. It's been like this for kids in every school since the beginning of time - unwritten rules governed by popular people and administered to less popular people; laws they didn't make and don't agree with but have to live by anyway like pecking orders, and seating assignments, who you can be with, who you can talk to, who is popular, who you're supposed to ignore. It's not fair – never was. But It's just the way it is.

Ricky spots Molly sitting at a table by herself reading a book. "And Molly?" he says pointing in her direction. "She's the smartest nerd of all. I need her help in Biology - so back off. Any questions?"

Since Andrew hasn't been inside these walls, or any kind of High School for that matter, well, Ricky's pecking order Popular kid-made rules don't apply. He squints, looks Ricky directly in and the eye, and says, *"'Yes, I got a question. Does Barry Manilow know you raid his wardrobe?'"*

The Geeks and Nerds giggle in shock.

"What? Who?" says Ricky grabbing Andrew by the collar. "You a wise ass, kid?"

Andrew finds an open Cheeto's bag alongside Skype's laptop. He reaches for one, holds it close to Ricky's face, and says menacingly, *"'See this? This is this. This ain't something else. This is this.'"*

"What? What the...? What the hell is he talking about?" Ricky asks the Nerds looking for an answer.

"You really are a freak, you know that?" he says giving Andrew a shove, then walks away, a little spooked and a lot confused.

The Nerds and Geeks look over from their table and give Andrew a confident thumbs up. He smiles to himself, feeling more and more confident using movie lines. 'This may not be so bad after all,' he thinks to himself.

He looks over at Molly, wanting so badly to go up and ask her if she saw his super cool act of bravery - but she is heads down quietly reading a book by herself, like always.

Skype slides a tray onto the table and plops beside him. "Molly Peterson?" he asks breaking Andrew's trance. "Honestly, dude, forget her. Not unless you've read, like, a million books. I heard she reads for, like, *pleasure.* You believe that? Who wants to read something that's not assigned? Besides, all those books become movies and then you can just download them."

Skype shovels a mound of greasy cafeteria food into his mouth and asks, "You like movies, kid?"

Andrew looks at Skype and just smiles - as if to say, 'Dude, you have no idea.'

JOHNSON HOUSE

****

The Johnson house a well-kept Dutch Colonial on a beautifully manicured tree-lined street. Inside, everything is neat and orderly. Clothes are folded in drawers. Dishes are cleaned and put away. The smell of a roasted chicken dinner wafts from the kitchen. It's everything the Wilden house wasn't.

"Mom, you called my phone like six times today," Skype yells entering the back door, just off the kitchen.

"Oh, stop. A mother can call her son any time she wants to," replies Mrs. Johnson playfully giving him a big fat smooch. Andrew stands beside him, uncomfortable and jealous, feeling like he doesn't belong.

"And who's this handsome young man?" she asks.

"This is Andrew, Mom."

"Very nice to meet you Andrew. Michael never has," but Mrs. Johnson catches herself. "I mean, he's usually not with..."

"I told you, my crew calls me Skype, Mom," he snaps before his mother can finish.

"Right....Skype," Mrs. Johnson says with a wink in Andrew's direction. It's easy to like her, she's so pleasant. "Got it. Well, would your 'crew' like something to eat?"

Andrew squints his eyes and asks, "'*You got any white bread?*'"

"Ah, yes. I...I think we do," replies a perplexed Mrs. Johnson.

"'*I'll have some toasted white bread, please, Ma'am,*'" says Andrew.

Now she is really lost.

Skype takes Andrew by the arm and escorts him upstairs. "Um, yeah, so...we're gonna go do some homework."

He turns back to his mother and says, "'*We're on a mission from God.*'"

****

A door swings open to a room filled with cameras, computers, Audio/Video equipment, and an enormous flat screen TV. The works.

"My brother is away at college, so I turned his room into my Man Cave," Skype tells him. "Pretty cool, right? Me and the

66

squad usually hang here. My boy David is always, like, 'Yo, my turn.' Then Tommy is like, 'No, man, me first.' Then, I'm like, 'Dudes, chill. Everyone gets a turn.' It can get a little...it's crazy...really," says Skype with a fake laugh, trying way too hard.

Andrew looks to the lone bean bag chair sitting in the middle of the room beside a single Xbox gaming controller. It's awkward.

Skype begins to admit sadly. "Yeah, well, I, um...I invite them, but...people usually have other plans and stuff. I get to come home to all of this, though. Watch what I want. Nobody to bother me."

Andrew knows exactly how that feels. He knows loneliness. He bends for the single game controller, squints his eyes and says, "'*Shall we play a game?*'"

"Do you always do that?" asks Skype.

"Do what?"

"Quote movie lines. That's from WAR GAMES, right?"

Andrew reflects for a moment, then admits slowly, "Sometimes it's easier to be somebody else, ya know?"

Skype knows exactly what he means. He's been trying to be the cool kid and act like nothing bothers him, not even the nickname that people gave to him in seventh grade – but it hurts. He looks at Andrew and asks, "Wanna see something really cool?"

Skype swings open a closet door and Andrew's eyes go wide as saucers. In front of him are rows and rows of movie DVD cases and VHS cassettes. It's as if he's home – if only for a brief moment.

Skype reaches for a copy of THE BLUES BROTHERS. He turns to Andrew and says, "'*You want jam on that dry white toast, Honey?*'"

Andrew smiles. So does Skype. Warm happy smiles. The smiles of someone who for the very first time has found a friend.

CHILD PROTECTIVE SERVICES

****

Claire is heads down shuffling through papers, unorganized as ever, when Jean Russell, her Supervisor for Bristol County Department of Children and Families appears in her office.

"We're gonna need to talk about the Wilden casefile. Is it true he's staying with the local police?" Supervisor Russell asks.

"Yes. Officer Muldoon," Claire responds, still looking through the mess. "It's only temporary."

"One of your 'small town, small rules' applicants? There's a protocol, Claire. I need to review the details."

"I'm sure it's here somewhere," replies Claire, frantically searching with absolutely no idea where anything is.

Supervisor Russell is losing patience. "Have you done a home study? Did it pass Physical Standards? Did you even perform a Background Check on Mr. Muldoon?"

Claire momentarily stops her search and looks up with feigned disbelief. "We went to High School together, Jean," she says with pointed firmness, trying to mask the fact that she didn't remember Danny Muldoon.

Jean Russell waits a moment before delivering this next part. She knows Claire is very good at what she does, and she's only trying to help. "A house just opened up in Fall River. All the proper application forms have been filled out."

"But Andrew is already enrolled in Somerset. His father is..."

Jean doesn't let her finish. "I spoke with the hospital, Claire. Mr. Wilden exhibited severe symptoms of paranoia and delusion. He'll need individual psychotherapy and Cognitive-Behavioral therapy - they need to make sure he's not a risk of hurting himself, or others. It could take months until his condition is stabilized. Maybe years."

Claire takes that all in.

"I'm sorry, but Andrew will need to be placed in proper, certified care - at least until he's eighteen," she says firmly. "I'll give you a couple weeks, but if there's nothing available locally...it's protocol, Claire. You really should know better."

Claire watches her leave, then goes back to frantic search mode looking for the missing casefile.

SOMERSET HIGH SCHOOL

****

Kids rush through the halls, heads down, earplugs in. Andrew is still struggling to open his vandalized locker. Skype reaches into his own locker, pulls out his brown bagged lunch and   looks at the contents.

"Carrots sticks? Celery? Baloney sandwich? Is she trying to kill me? At least she gave me gum. Never know when you'll need minty fresh breath. Am I right ladies?" he says to the passing trio of Plastics.

They ignore him - like always.

He sighs and slumps against the locker. "Just once I'd like to be invited to one of their parties. I'd like to be invited anywhere."

He reaches back into the brown paper bag and pulls out a small yellow sticky note.

"What's that?" asks Andrew.

"My mother leaves a note in my lunch every day," he says not masking his embarrassment. Andrew shakes his head, thinking how much he wished his mother was around to leave

72

him little yellow sticky notes, and gum, and celery sticks, and baloney sandwiches in little brown paper bags.

Skype reads aloud, "Let's see what we have today. *'The question isn't who is going to let me; it's who is going to stop me.'*" He turns to Andrew. "Seriously? What does that even mean?"

"That's Ayn Rand," says Molly overhearing the conversation a few lockers away.

Skype's face contorts. "Who?"

"Ayn Rand," repeats Molly. "She's a Russian novelist. The Fountainhead? Atlas Shrugged?"

Of course, they don't recognize the books. Who would ever read a book for pleasure?!

"Cool," smirks Skype with a bob of his head. "I could be into Russian chicks. Here are your Shakespeare notes."

"You used your own ideas, right? Original thought, remember?" Molly implores.

Before Skype can answer, he gets bumped into the lockers accidentally/on purpose by ...you guessed it, Ricky and the Sidekicks. His brown lunch bag falls to the ground spilling the gum, notebook, and sandwich onto the cold linoleum floor. Skype gives an exaggerated 'here we go again' eye roll.

"Sorry, my man," laughs over-sized jock Ricky. "Didn't see you there."

The Sidekicks laugh and high-five. (like always)

"Is that my homework down there?" asks Ricky spotting the fallen notebook.

"No. It's...it's Molly's," Skype tells him.

"Ooh. Even better," says Ricky bending to get her notes. Molly leans to Skype. "Why do you let him push you around?"

"Please," Skype whispers back. "I have a reputation. I'm the King of Backing Down. Just let him get it out of his system."

As Ricky reaches for the notebook, a foot promptly steps on it. He looks up. It's Andrew.

Ricky's face turns red. For a moment he resembles Vern Gleason - the blood pressure Gleason, not the psoriasis /rosacea Gleason. He grabs Andrew by the shirt and turns to the Sidekicks. "This is the kid I was telling you about. He acts like a freak, talks like a freak, and hangs out with a freak. I think he needs a lesson on who runs things around here, boys."

Andrew stands firm and strong. He looks Ricky in the eye, squints and says, "'*Just you and me. Two hits. Me hitting you, you hitting the floor.*'"

Ricky is surprised by Andrew's confidence. He doesn't want to back down, not in front of everyone. They glare, nose to nose, ready to fight. The situation could go either way. Suddenly, Mr. Gleason is walking in their direction. "Is there a problem here, gentlemen?"

"Not yet," snarls Ricky through gritted teeth releasing his grip. He looks to the spilled lunch items on the floor, and with a nod of his head, instructs the Sidekicks.

"Leave the gum. Take the baloney."

Skype and Andrew share a deadpan look. Seriously? Nobody else gets that Godfather reference?

Molly bends to retrieve her notebook. Andrew rushes to help. Their hands touch and their eyes meet for a moment, but this time it's not awkward. In fact, there is such an unmistakable current between them that their touching fingers almost ignite.

Andrew speaks softly, "'*Arise, fair sun, and kill the envious moon, that thou, her maid, art far more fair than she.*'"

Molly doesn't realize it, but she's blushing.

"Th - thank you," she stammers, mesmerized, and stumbles away, looking back with each step. She turns and smiles to herself. It's the kind of bright, curious smile that stays inside of her for days.

Skype leans to Andrew. "So, you're quoting William Shakespeare now?"

"Who?" he replies genuinely confused. "I thought that was Leonardo DiCaprio."

POLICE STATION

****

Muldoon punches numbers into the phone on his desk. It's clear by his reaction that he's getting a familiar voice recording indicating the person on the other end is not there. He hangs up, frustrated, and makes a note in a manila folder under the heading: **ALLISON WILDEN**

He calls out to Kobolowski standing by the coffee machine. "Hey, can you still get tickets to the Sox games? Thought I'd take Andrew. I don't know if he's ever been to Fenway."

"I doubt it. Kid's never been anywhere," replies Kobolowski. He hands Muldoon a coffee and sits beside the desk. "The old man was what they call a 'Quant' - sort of the rocket scientists of Wall Street. I guess he was a real wiz at math and statistics. Worked at Morgan Stanley for years."

He stirs the coffee, then raises his eyes. "His office used to be across from the World Trade Center."

Silence. Muldoon leans in, listening intently.

"After 9/11, Wilden packed up and left the city. Can't really blame him. Moved the family to Somerset and opened the video store. I interviewed a bunch of his old customers. They say he was always a bit quirky, but after Sandy Hook, and then the Marathon bombing - well, he got real bad. Wouldn't let the wife or kid ever leave the house. Only for a few strictly monitored trips to the store. Didn't want them on the 'nefarious streets' he called them."

"Nefarious? Somerset?" replies Muldoon.

"I know, right?" says Kobolowski leaning back in his chair and sipping at the coffee. "And you get talked into keeping his kid. You are hopeless Muldoon."

"It's only temporary. She's really persuasive," he admits quietly. "Always was."

Kobolowski sits up. "Was? Wait, you know her?"

"We went to High School together," Muldoon admits. "Only, she doesn't remember me."

"Who could forget a smooth talker like you?" his partner says with a laugh. Kobolowski's eyes narrow. "Wait a minute. Oh, Danny Boy. You like her. I can tell."

"No, I don't," Muldoon replies, almost too fast. "I don't know. I used to. Maybe."

"How are you ever gonna get a girl if you let them push you around?" his partner tells him. "You need to know how to _not_ talk to a woman. Take me and Angela. I haven't had a real conversation with my wife since 1987. *Lack of communication.* Say nah-thing. It's the key to a good marriage. 'Ooh, my feelings. My emotional journey.' In my house, I'm the boss. I wear the pants."

Muldoon rolls his eyes at Kobolowski's bravado as their co-worker, Caroline Butler walks by to grab a coffee.

"Hey, guys."

Muldoon is immediately tongue tied. He sits up straight and goes back to 'Cop-speak' mode. "Good morning, Officer Butler. We were, ah, just retrieving our caffeinated beverage."

She knows Muldoon is a mess around women. "It's fine," Officer Butler says, playfully mocking him. "I'm just 'retrieving a caffeinated beverage' myself."

Danny Muldoon has absolutely zero game with women.

SOMERSET HIGH SCHOOL

****

Andrew and Skype walk through the Somerset High parking lot past shiny new Range Rovers, and oversized Suburbans - cars with the perfect amount of status for the Plastic's egos, and truck space for the Jock's sports equipment. The cars sit in stark contrast to the worn Chevy Novas and leased Kias that belong to their Public School salaried teachers.

"So, you talk to Molly yet?" Skype asks. "You know, as 'Normal Guy Andrew' not 'Movie Guy Andrew'?"

"Trust me," Andrew replies. "'Movie Guy Andrew' is way cooler. And a lot more interesting,'"

"Of course that Andrew is more interesting," Skype tells him. "She's never seen any of those movies."

"Wait, seriously?"

"Yep, I heard she doesn't even have a television. Can you believe that? This day and age? It's child abuse, that's what that is."

Molly jogs towards them across the lot.

"Hey guys," she says, a bit breathless. "Andrew. Hi. Um, my mom wanted to know... well, she thought it might be a good givesidea...do you wanna come over? I mean, I have all my Biology notes at home, and, well, I was thinking, since we're lab partners and everything."

Andrew tries to contain his excitement. Skype stops dead in his tracks. "Wait...w   hat about all that 'original thought and think for yourself stuff?'"

She gives an innocent shrug, then looks at Andrew. "So, four o'clock?"

Andrew smirks, squints his eyes, and says, "'*I was just gonna say - four o'clock.*'"

She takes off, walking on air. Skype punches Andrew playfully on the arm. "Dude, she's all smitten and stuff. '*You're my density.*'"

"You do realize the girl in BACK TO THE FUTURE was his mother, right?" Andrew tells him.

"I know. Totally messed up. But she was still kinda hot, right?" Skype replies.

Andrew punches him on the arm - a little too hard based on Skype's dramatic overreaction.

PETERSON HOUSE

****

Andrew wanders through the Peterson living room, his fingers brushing past each book piled on the floor and filling the shelves. History. Poetry. Autobiography. Fiction. Everything he would ever want to read is there at his fingertips, all inside a cluttered Victorian home in Somerset. It's an eerily resemblance of when he would roam his parent's video store as a child.

"Can I get you anything to eat?" asks Molly.

"*'You got any dry white...'*" Andrew begins, but stops himself. "No. Um, thank you. I'm good."

His eyes scan the room. Something is missing. Molly knows what he's looking for.

"Yeah, um, we don't have a television. Pretty lame, right? We obviously do a lot of reading around here."

"No, I think that's really cool," Andrew tells her.

"Thanks," replies Molly, her admiration and fondness for him growing.

Andrew spots Ben sitting in the adjacent playroom, engrossed in his Legos and toy dinosaurs.

"That's my brother," Molly says cheerfully. "Ben, this is Andrew."

There's no response, no eye contact. Ben just rocks gently back and forth, stimming, lining up his toys in symmetrical patterns. Molly can sense Andrew's curiosity. She leans close and whispers, "He's kinda...well, he can be a little...bizarre."

Andrew doesn't miss a beat. He looks Molly directly in the eye and says; "'*We're all pretty bizarre. Some of us are just better at hiding it, that's all.*'"

Molly takes that in as if Andrew has just spoken the most profound words she has ever heard.

There is something about Ben, something that draws Andrew close. Maybe it's Ben's sense of loneliness, of being trapped in his own world. Maybe it's the gentle rocking that reminds him of his father as he sat huddled on the bedroom floor. Maybe Andrew just sees a little bit of himself. He approaches, but Molly intervenes "Don't. He really doesn't like it when people..."

But Andrew isn't listening, he's kneeling beside Ben.

Molly watches with wonder as Ben hands Andrew a Lego piece. They sit and quietly begin to clip the pieces together. Molly is amazed. It's the first time she has ever seen her little brother make a connection with someone.

JOHNSON HOUSE

****

Skype sits at the computer in his Man Cave, scrolling through the internet. He lands on a personal YouTube page that holds a list of videos he's made with his cell phone. Most of them are Skype roaming the halls of Somerset High saying things like, "Whaddup Ladies!" and "Yo, my man!" only to have a hand thrown in front of the camera telling him to back off or get away.

There are several clips of Skype offering witty observations about school and teachers and society and pecking orders of Plastics and Jocks. They're good. Really good. And funny, too. But no one has ever seen them.

The top right side of the page shows his total subscribers. It's eight. These include his mother, his father, his older brother, four of Mrs. Johnson's close friends, and some random weird dude in Texas who keeps messaging Skype to chat.

Skype toggles the cursor between the PRIVATE and PUBLIC icons, deciding whether to finally publish the videos. He thinks for a moment. Should I do it? Should I make them public so everyone can see how funny I am? How observant and witty I am? How cool I can be if you just let me? Maybe they'll see that I'm not a Freak, or a Nerd, or a Geek, or a Loser!

He pulls the arrow icon away. Forget it. Maybe tomorrow.

CLICK. The screen changes to his Facebook page. He scrolls the curser over the FIND FRIENDS icon.

There are NO NEW FRIEND REQUESTS. He moves the icon to VIEW SENT REQUESTS. No one has accepted his requests.

He sadly closes the laptop just as Mrs. Johnson enters. She can tell something is up with her son. Mothers always know.

"That boy the other day seemed nice," she says with a soft, loving tone.

"Yeah, he's pretty cool. He's the one I told you about. His parents and everything," Skype replies.

"Such a shame," says the kind-hearted Mrs. Johnson. "Well, you tell Andrew he is welcome here any time. OK?"

"I will, Mom. Thanks."

Mrs. Johnson walks over and kisses her lonely son on the forehead.

MULDOON'S APARTMENT

****

Muldoon enters the apartment carrying pizza and groceries to find Andrew staring at a blank television screen, his father's black remote control firmly in his hand.

"You can turn that on. It works. You just....you need to use this one though," Muldoon tells him tossing the new remote into Andrew's lap.

"So...how was, ah, how was school?" Muldoon asks.

No response.

"I'm not a big talker myself," Muldoon continues as he puts the groceries away and opens the pizza box. "Miss Peterson probably told you that. Did, ah, did she...did she say anything about me at all?"

He eagerly awaits a reply. Nothing from Andrew.

"Not really sure what teenagers talk about these days. My day, it was all about girls. And beer. I'm a police officer now, so I guess we better just keep it to girls. OK?"

Still nothing. Muldoon stops what he's doing, looks in Andrew's direction and lowers his voice. *"'You know, it's legal*

for me to take you down to the station and sweat it out of you
under the lights.'"

Andrew looks up, recognizing the line.

"I'm just kidding. That's from a movie or something," says Muldoon breaking into a smile.

Yeah. Andrew knows.

"I only have one question," Muldoon says. "Sausage or pepperoni?"

"Pepperoni," says Andrew softly.

Finally, a connection! Muldoon slaps the pizza on the table and opens the fridge. "Cool. Now, let's see if we can go two for two. Root beer or Coke?"

"Root beer," says Andrew.

"Ok, here we go," cheers Muldoon. "I don't know what Kobolowski was talking about. I can communicate."

Thrilled with the minor victory, he grabs a slice.

"So, you wanna watch a movie or something?" asks Muldoon with a mouthful of pizza.

"I could go for a movie," Andrew replies feeling more comfortable.

Muldoon takes the remote and starts to flip through the channels, talking incessantly and thinking out loud with each channel CLICK.

"I was never a good talker," he begins.

CLICK

"I'm even worse with girls."

CLICK

"Claire especially."

CLICK

"She was so intimidating in High School. I mean, I used to get all tongue tied around her."

CLICK

"Still do."

CLICK

"How are you supposed to communicate with a woman like that?"

CLICK.

"'Lack of communication.' What does that even mean?"

CLICK

"Women are complicated, aren't they? I don't know what they want."

CLICK

"Do you know what they want?"

Andrew rolls his eyes. 'Jeeze,' he thinks, 'for someone who doesn't communicate, this guy hasn't shut up!'

Muldoon finally stops changing channels and lands on a movie. Ryan Gosling is wooing Rachel McAdams in THE NOTEBOOK.

Muldoon watches for a few seconds, then looks at Andrew as if to say, 'I'll watch this if you want to.' Andrew nods back with a nonchalant 'I will if you will' shrug.

There is the simultaneous hiss of cans - Budweiser for Muldoon, Root beer for Andrew - as the two roommates settle in to watch the sappy love story.

SOMERSET HIGH SCHOOL

****

It was always assumed that Ricky Sherman would get a football scholarship. His brother got a full ride to play at the University of Rhode Island. His sister got tuition reimbursement to play field hockey as Assumption. His father was a two-way starter for UMass and made the scout team with the Giants. His mother received grant money for being a scholar athlete at Stonehill. So, when Ricky started struggling with his grades in middle school, he did the only thing he could think of to get better test scores – cheat. Study harder? Focus more? Pay attention? No way. And there was no way in hell he would ever let his parents meet with the teachers to try and get him help. Every kid knows that when a parent is seen in the hallways of school at 3:30 in the afternoon they're there because you're in trouble or because they have an IEP meeting. God forbid your friends see them. 'C's get degree's' became Ricky's motto. Just do enough to keep getting by - and when that doesn't work out, bully someone into doing the work for you.

So, instead of getting embarrassed by bad test scores, Ricky got angry. Then he got mean. And those emotions helped him on the Friday night football fields all over Bristol County.

Players from rival towns like Fall River and Taunton and Rehoboth felt Ricky Sherman's emotion. Some even have the scars and casts to prove it.

Ricky just needs to keep those grades to an average level if he has any hope of following in the Sherman family scholarship tradition. Since he failed to hand in Mr. Gleason's homework assignment, getting a C in that class seems like it will be a stretch. So....

Ricky looks up and down the school hallway making sure the coast is clear. He sneaks into Mr. Gleason's empty classroom, then, c   hecking around to make sure the coast is clear, he slowly removes a stack of papers from the top drawer, holds his cell phone up and snaps a photo of the mid-term exam questions.

As he slides the papers back in place, Ricky notices a folder marked **ANDREW WILDEN**. He opens it, begins to read the file, and his eyes go wide.

A bell rings. He quickly tosses the folder back into the drawer just before Mr. Gleason enters the room

"Mister Sherman," Mr. Gleason exclaims. "Nice to see you arrive early for once. I hope you're preparing for the mid-term?"

Ricky replies with a sinister smirk.   "Oh, I should be all set, Mr. Gleason. I sort of have a 'photographic' memory."

POLICE STATION

****

"Need to show you something," grunts Kobolowski placing a large brown cardboard box marked **EVIDENCE** onto Muldoon's desk. "We found this hidden in the back of Allison Wilden's closet."

Muldoon stands and begins to review the contents. A concerned look forms on his face. "Has Andrew seen this?"

"No. I figured you'd want to go through it first," his partner replies.

Officer Butler yells from across the station. "Kobolowski, your wife is on the phone."

"Tell her I'm busy," Kobolowski yells back full of feigned machismo.

"Tell her yourself," snaps Officer Butler. She's used to working with old school machismo guys like Kobolowski. Carol Butler isn't one to be ordered around. "You better hurry. She sounds mad."

Kobolowski's face is suddenly wracked with fear. His whole demeanor changes as he lovingly speaks into the phone.

"Hi honey...Yes, yes Dear...Of course not... I'm sorry sweetie. No, my love...I will...I...I... gotta go. Bye."

Officer Butler looks at Muldoon and smirks, "Who wears the pants?"

But Muldoon doesn't respond. He's too busy reviewing items inside the box belonging to Allison Wilden – and he is deeply troubled by its contents.

PETERSON HOUSE

****

The doorbell rings. Claire is surprised to see Danny Muldoon standing at her front door.

"Afternoon, Ma'am...I mean, Claire. I was told Andrew was here? He's been studying with your daughter..." he nervously refers to the notepad in his breast pocket. "Molly?"

"Danny. Hello. Andrew is at the Johnsons with Skype. But, come in. I can get you a coffee this time."

"No, thank you. I'm taking the boys to a Red Sox game."

Being super nosey, Nana May pokes her head around the corner and eyes Muldoon up and down. "Claire, you didn't tell me it was Daniel Muldoon. You two went to High School together."

"Yeah. I know, Mom. *Jeeze!*" says Claire with an exaggerated eye roll, once again deflecting the fact she didn't remember.

"I was so sorry to hear about your mother, Daniel," Nana May tells him. "She was a wonderful lady."

"Thank you, Ma'am."

"Ma'am?" says Nana May, looking directly at Claire. "Oh, so this is the man you were going on about. *'Ma'am'* this. All *'official'* that. If I didn't know better, I'd think my daughter had a schoolgirl crush."

Claire is mortified. Muldoon turns bright red.

"Call me Nana May. Short for Maya - my Hindu name. It means Magic," she says waving her arms with a flourish.

Claire whispers, "Her real name is Martha."

Nana May grabs Muldoon by the arm. "Come in, Daniel. I insist."

"No, thank you Ma'...Nana May."

"Nonsense," she says practically dragging Muldoon into the house. The dogs immediately surround him, tails wagging, tongues licking.

Muldoon notices Ben in the corner of the room quietly playing with his Legos and dinosaurs and approaches to introduce himself.

"Afternoon, son. How you doin' there?"

No answer. Muldoon looks to Claire and asks, "Does your son like baseball? I'd be happy to take him along."

"No, thank you," replies Claire.

"I don't mind, really," he says.

"I really don't think it's a good idea," Claire tells him.

"Oh, I think that's a great idea!" interjects Nana May.

Claire's eyes shoot daggers at her mother.

Muldoon insists, trying too hard. "Really. It's no problem at all."

"No, thank you. Ben has a routine," Claire says a bit firmer.

"Claire. Let him go," pleads Nana May.

"The station gets plenty of tickets," Muldoon goes on. "You could all come."

"Oh, wouldn't that be fun!" exclaims Nana May.

Muldoon approaches Ben. "Every kid likes baseball. Ben is it? Come on, Ben, let's..." he says reaching out for Ben's hand.

Claire reacts. Hard. Too hard. "I said no. Enough! I don't want him to go!"

Muldoon stops in his tracks, confused and shaken. Ben suddenly cries out, upset by Claire's outburst. Nana May rushes to comfort him, her face full of disappointment at her daughter's behavior. An uncomfortable tension hangs over the room.

"I... I'm sorry," says Muldoon, confused and embarrassed. "I didn't mean to...Of course, Ma'am. I'm so sorry, Ben. Mrs....Nana... Well, I'll just...I better go get the boys."

Muldoon can't get out of there fast enough. Claire feels badly and motions towards the door to go after him. She should apologize, explain her situation, her life, how organized she use to be, how some days she just can't seem to get out of her own way...but she doesn't. She just watches Danny Muldoon get in his squad car and drive away.

JOHNSON HOUSE

****

Andrew sits alone in Skype's bedroom, waiting for him to return from the basement after Mrs. Johnson made him finally, *mercifully*, pick up that dirty laundry. He scans items on a shelf above the computer. There are seashells from trips to the beach, pictures from a vacation to Disney World, spelling trophies Skype won in grade school. It's all the things Andrew never got to experience. His eyes land on a Johnson family photo of Skype, his parents and older brother. The perfect happy family.

Andrew turns to the computer and CLICKS the screen to open Skype's Facebook page. He moves the curser to the search bar, and types ALLISON WILDEN. An assortment of profiles appears. Andrew quickly scrolls the pages. None of them are his mother.

He minimizes Facebook, and Skype's YouTube page pops on screen with the list of short movies and clips. Andrew moves the curser to CLICK when --

"Don't touch that!" is screamed from across the room. Skype races over to minimize the page. "You almost posted them!"

"Did you make these movies?" Andrew asks. "They look pretty cool."

Skype shrugs and tries to deflect the hurt, "They would only get, like, ten views anyway."

After a moment, he confesses quietly, "Do you know I only have fourteen followers on Instagram? Most of them are my family - and a few weirdos. I send out friend requests on Facebook but..." He pauses, realizing the severity and hurt of sharing this sad truth aloud for the first time. "I see all the pictures they post. Birthday parties. Trips to the mall. Everyone hanging at a friend's house. Do you know why they call me Skype?"

"I figured it's because of all your computers and stuff," Andrew replies.

"I got sick in seventh grade. Had to spend most of the year at home. They set up a computer and put a camera in the classroom so I could see the teacher and the board and stuff. You know - Skype. I was stuck in my room the whole time. I could still hear the kids. Talking. Laughing. Every now and then someone would stick tape on the lens so I couldn't see, or bump the camera so it was pointed to the floor"

He pauses to collect himself, staring at the computer as if he needed support and answers, the pain of the past unearthed. "Do you have any idea what it's like to watch your whole world through a stupid little screen?"

Andrew knows exactly how that feels.

"You'll never know unless you put yourself out there," Andrew tells him.

"Yo, Crew," shouts Mrs. Johnson standing in the doorway. "Officer Muldoon is downstairs. He's very...*official*, isn't he?" she says with a smirk.

"Wear your jackets, it's going to be chilly," says the over-protective-mother. "And remember to have fun, you two."

Mrs. Johnson lovingly kisses her son on the forehead. Then she leans down and kisses Andrew on the forehead too - and he beams.

FENWAY PARK

****

It's a cool Spring night in Boston for a Red Sox game, the air is fat with the smell of Italian sausage, grilled onions and stale beer. Andrew and Skype sit along the third base line eating hot dogs, chewing pretzels, drinking sugary soda. With every pitch, they rattle baseball movie lines back and forth, cracking each other up - and bugging the living shit outta Officer Muldoon.

"'*Juuuust a bit outside*,'" yells Skype.

"'*Pick me out a winner, Bobby*,'" replies Andrew.

"'*You're killing me, Smalls. You're killing me*'!"

"'*There's no crying in baseball!*'"

"'*Hey batta batta hey batta batta batta SWING batta!*'"

Muldoon has had enough. "Oh my God, stop!" He looks at Andrew. "First, I can't get you to talk, now you won't shuddap!"

The teenagers bust out laughing. They are having the time of their lives.

"What's with you guys and the movie lines?" Muldoon asks. "Can't you just talk like a normal person, for crying out loud?"

Skype looks at Muldoon. "Can't you?"

"What's that supposed to mean?" he asks.

"Please, I've seen you around Molly's mom. You're hopeless, dude," Skype tells him. *"Yes, Ma'am. No, Ma'am. That's a 10-57, Ma'am.* You're all, like, RoboCop and stuff."

Andrew laughs, *"Serve the public, protect the innocent, uphold the law."*

Muldoon tries to brush it off. "Oh, like you guys would know how to talk to a girl."

After a moment, he asks - almost pleading, "Do you guys know how to talk to a girl?"

"Trust me," says Skype full of confidence. "Girls love movies more than guys. You want to impress a girl? Tell her you felt sorry for Katniss Everdeen in HUNGER GAMES but respect her strength and courage. Or, admit you watched A WALK IN THE CLOUDS all the way through. And if you really want them to fall for you? Tell them you cried during THE NOTEBOOK."

Muldoon and Andrew immediately look at each other as if to say, 'I didn't cry!'

"So, you guys really think watching movies could help?" Muldoon asks.

The friends look at each other. Their eyes suddenly widen as an idea forms - and they begin to hatch a plan.

CHAPTER II

MULDOON'S APARTMENT

****

Andrew Wilden stands beside a tall AV cart, the metal shelf just below the TV has an assortment of VHS cassette tapes. Classic Romantic Comedies like SAY ANYTHING, ANNIE HALL, PRINCESS BRIDE. He addresses his 'pupil' with a long wooden pointer in one hand and a black remote control in the other.

"Alright, class. Settle in. Let's see what we have today. Ooh, Social Studies," Andrew says sliding a cassette from its sleeve. He reads aloud, "WHEN HARRY MET SALLY - Rob Reiner's touching Romantic Comedy that begs the question, can men be friends with women without wanting sex."

Skype and Muldoon immediately look at each other. This is going to be interesting.

The cassette is inserted into the VCR, and class begins. On the television screen, Billy Crystal speaks to Meg Ryan in a silly accent.

"'*Waiter, there is too much pepper on my paprikash.*'"

Meg Ryan repeats the line. "'*Waiter, there is too much pepper on my paprikash.*'"

"'But I would be proud to partake of your pecan pie.'"

Muldoon sits at a desk furiously taking notes, like an athlete studying game film.

Skype looks at Andrew with a confident smirk and says, "A vast wasteland, my ass."

SOMERSET, MA

****

Andrew and Skype sit in the front seat of Mrs. Johnson's mini-van, face to face, eye to eye. There is a seriousness in the air as they each take a deep breath.

"You sure about this?" Andrew asks.

"Never been surer of anything in my life," says an overly confident Skype.

"I don't know," replies a reluctant Andrew.

"Listen to me," Skype tells him. "You've studied hours of DVD. Memorized miles of VHS tape. Play, rewind, play, rewind again, all in preparation for this very moment. My son, you are ready." He pauses, then says, " *There is no try. Only do.*"

Andrew takes a deep breath, nods, and slowly begins to clap. CLAP...CLAP...CLAP...

Skype immediately waves him off. "No. No. We're not...we're not doing the slow clap thing."

****

In a quick passage of time, Andrew takes Molly on a series of dates, each one a re-enactment of a famous scene from some Romantic Comedy. Since Molly has never seen the movies, she thinks Andrew is the most romantic, thoughtful, funny and original boy she has ever met.

PRETTY WOMAN - Skype drives the Johnson's minivan, terrified his mother will kill them both if she ever finds out since he only has his learner's permit. He slouches down low and drives past Molly walking home from school. Andrew suddenly pops his head through the sunroof and hands her a red rose.

SAY ANYTHING - Molly sits in her room doing homework. The Peter Gabriel song 'In Your Eyes' blares from outside. She runs to the window to see Andrew standing on her front lawn. He's wearing a long brown trench coat and holds a boom box over his head as the music plays on.

114

THE NOTEBOOK - Andrew and Molly sit in a row boat in the middle of Clear Pond, gazing into each other's eyes. Hidden in the bushes by the water's edge is Skype, ready to recreate the romantic lake scene - only instead of swans, he has little plastic yellow rubber duckies.

A rubber duck floats by the row boat. And another. Then several. Then hundreds. Molly and Andrew's rowboat is literally surrounded by floating yellow rubber ducks – and Molly is loving it.

Mission accomplished, Skype turns to leave - and bumps straight into Officer Kobolowski. He is _so_ busted.

TITANIC - Andrew gingerly walks Molly along the edge of a railing. He removes her blindfold to reveal a majestic view overlooking all of Somerset. Molly is at first nervous, but Andrews holds her close. They lean over the edge, wind blowing in their face. Andrew stands on the railing and screams like Jack Dawson, *"I'm the king of the world."*

SIXTEEN CANDLES - Molly and Andrew sit cross-legged on top of a table, a cake with lit candles between them. They look deeply into each other's eyes, just like Samantha and Jake did in the movie. They are falling in love.

POLICE STATION

****

"Can I help you?" Officer Caroline Butler asks Claire.

"I'm looking for Officer Muldoon," she replies standing in the lobby of the station with two cups of coffee.

"What's this regarding?"

"It's a Protective Services matter," Claire tells her. "Kinda private. I really would like to speak with him."

Kobolowski spots Claire from the back of the station and rushes to alert Muldoon. "Yo, the Peterson woman is here," he tells him with a hushed whisper.

Muldoon is terrified. "Claire? Here? What? I mean, why is she here?"

"I don't know," his partner replies. "Listen to me...Nah-thing. Say nah-thing. Lack of communication. Got it?"

Claire approaches the desk. "Hi, Danny. I thought I'd bring you a coffee this time."

Kobolowski makes his way behind her, miming the words "Nah-thing!" behind her back to Muldoon.

"I got you black. I didn't have intel on how you take it," she says, gently mocking him.

Kobolowski is still behind her, dramatically waving his arms and urging Muldoon not to respond. Claire glances back. He's bagged, like a kid caught with his hand in the cookie jar.

"Anyway," Claire turns back to Muldoon." I wanted to apologize...about the other day...with Ben."

Muldoon stays strong and says nothing. Lack of communication. He's got this. Claire's mood shifts.

"You do realize I get the silent treatment enough at home, right?"

Muldoon looks over her shoulder to Kobolowski. His eye bugging out as if to say, Stay strong Dan!

"Well," Claire finally relents. "Enjoy your coffee. I am sorry." And she's gone.

After a moment, Muldoon regrets his actions and takes off   .

"I'm sorry about that" he says, out of breath, catching up just before she gets into her car.

"Me too."

Claire can't stay mad at him – he's too nice a guy, and too darn cute. She is as smitten as her teenage daughter.

"Could we just sit and talk?" she asks. Muldoon's face goes pale.

****

If Danny Muldoon kept his own list of The Most Terrifying Things in the World, it would be:

1. Spiders
2. Snakes
3. Heights
4. Finding a Seat in the High School Cafeteria.
5. Sit and Talk to a Girl

Claire and Muldoon find a nearby park bench and sit in silence.

"I'm sorry. It's been really crazy lately, and I took it out on you," she says then turns her body to face him with a look of concern. "I'm getting pressure to relocate Andrew."

"But...but why?" he asks, stunned. "We're doing fine."

"I know," Claire reassures him. "Any luck at all with the mother?"

118

"No," Muldoon tells her. "He has an uncle, but he's overseas doing some kind of private contracting for the military. He and the father haven't talked in years. The mother was an only child. Both sets of parents have passed away. So, no grandparents, no aunts, no cousins. Nothing."

Claire breathes a heavy sigh. She knows it's out of her control at this point.

"Andrew is going to need more permanent care. If not with family, then with people that are certified," she tells him. "I'm sorry, Danny, but it's protocol."

"Protocol," Muldoon repeats the word. He looks off, genuinely sad. Sad for Andrew. Sad for himself.

"He keeps asking about his father."

Claire nods. "I know. I'm working on it. Some days I feel like I can't get out of my own way. It's always something."

She leans back on the bench and stares up to the sky, searching for answers or guidance or a sign – something, anything.

"Unicorn notebooks and colored pens," she says with a sad kind of laugh. "I was organized in High School, wasn't I? I had everything planned. College. Marriage. Kids. Then one day my three-year-old suddenly stops talking. I knew something was wrong, mothers just know. They told me it was Regressive Autism. Ben was trapped in a sort of neurological prison - like he just vanished."

She pauses to collect herself and looks at her hands.

"My husband couldn't deal. Here was this accomplished physician and he can't even communicate with his own son."

Muldoon doesn't know what to say, or how to help. Claire continues, trying to lighten the mood a bit.

"I should've known we were doomed from the start. We met when we were in school. I was a Loyola Jesuit school girl and he was a Hopkins research nerd. Ben was just his convenient escape clause. So, he starts a new practice and a new family in California, and I'm stuck in Baltimore. I tried to make it work, enrolled Ben at Kennedy Kreiger, the top school in the country for kids with Autism. They started him on a round the clock regimen of speech and language therapies, behavioral therapies. He was sleeping maybe four hours a night. I was probably getting two or three tops. It was all taking its toll."

Muldoon can see she's hurting. "Must be nice to be back home, though. Your mom. Old friends."

"Yeah, well...I thought coming back to a small town could fix everything. It doesn't," she sadly admits.

Muldoon nods his head, realizing how those plans didn't work out for James Wilden either.

"My mother's been great," continues Claire. "But we don't exactly see eye to eye when it comes to Ben. She thinks if I just light candles and breathe through my nose, everything will be fine."

Muldoon laughs. "Ha. I remember your mom. She was always a bit out there. Can I ask? Why isn't Ben in school?"

"I had him in school for a while but...he had behavioral issues and would lash out. I was pretty much told to put him in an institution."

She looks to Muldoon, as if seeking his approval, and trying to convince herself. "But, I figured, if he's happy? If he's not hurting himself? Who better to help him than his family, right?"

Muldoon wants to take her hand, hold her, kiss her, anything to show her how much he cares. But he just nods and continues to listen.

"I used to beat myself up. Did I miss something? Did I do something? Did I _not_ do something? The world can be really cruel. Going places got to be difficult. Ben would draw stares in stores, restaurants. He looks fine, doesn't look like he has special needs...but, when he's behaving badly...well, clearly that's bad parenting, right? Control your son, right?"

She does her best to hold back her tears, and her anger.

"I just got so tired - all the misconceptions and unwanted advice. Say your kid has cancer and people line up to bring you dinners. But your kid acts up in the grocery store because he's on the spectrum? Everyone just thinks you're a terrible mother."

Muldoon's mood changes. He turns to face Claire and look her in the eye because this is important. "You're not a bad mother, Claire. You didn't just give up and leave."

There's a real bitterness in his voice. They both know he's talking about Allison Wilden.

"Raising a family on your own," Muldoon tells her. "Helping stray kids. Taking in stray dogs. Heck, you even find lost dinosaurs."

That finally makes Claire smile. "I just want these kids to see all the amazing possibilities that are ahead of them. Life is full of surprises, right?"

Muldoon smiles back. "Right."

Claire closes her eyes, Zen/Nana May style, and takes a deep breath - in through the nose, out through the mouth.

"If Ben would just let me hug him. That would be the greatest gift."

Muldoon spots an opportunity. Remembering his 'lessons' from Andrew, he channels Billy Crystal in WHEN HARRY MET SALLY and begins to speak with a silly accent.

"*'Would you like to go to the movies with me tonight?'*"

Claire is totally confused. "What? Why...why are you talking like that?"

"*'Would you like to...'*" He stops and goes back to his own voice. "Sorry. Um, would you like to go to the movies with me tonight?"

Claire is a bit taken aback. "Oh. I ...I don't think that's a good idea."

"I understand," replies Muldoon trying to mask his disappointment.

"No," says Claire. "It's just that…well, Ben has a routine and…"

"Sure. Some other time."

"We could do dinner?" Claire asks.

"Dinner?" he asks, his voice raised a pitch too high.

"Yeah. My house. I could cook," she tells him.

"Dinner," Muldoon repeats, the terror in his voice palpable. "Sure. Um, dinner would be good."

Danny Muldoon just added Number Six to his 'Most Terrifying Things in the World' list:

6.   Have Dinner with a Girl.

****

While Claire and Muldoon sit on the park bench, both terrified about the night that lays ahead, Andrew is back at Muldoon's apartment. He stands by the AV cart and reads the sleeve of a VHS cassette aloud to someone in the room.

"Ok, so today we have Disney's animated classic BAMBI. The heartwarming story of a young deer who lost his mother. He makes friends with the other animals, learns skills to survive on his own, and even falls in love."

Andrew reflects on that, then takes a seat.

The glow of the television screen flickers to life.

"See," says Andrew to the person beside him. "Everything you need is in the movies."

But he's starting to realize that's not true.

POLICE STATION

****

"Dinner?!" Kobolowski shouts at his partner. "I thought you said you were gonna go to the movies? Dinner means conversation. Talking. Chit-chat. Oh, you're screwed, Danny Boy."

"I know," says Muldoon, his shoulders slumped, realizing that he would prefer dinner with spiders, or snakes, in a cafeteria, high on a mountain.

"Say nothing," Kobolowski tells him. "Nah-thing. Let her do all the talking."

"I can't do this. I'm gonna need some help," Muldoon says with desperation and reaches for the phone.

****

Skype is alone in the Man Cave watching FAST TIMES AT RIDGEMONT HIGH when his cell phone rings.

"Talk to me...Yo, RoboCop what's up?...Nope, Andrew's not here, he's at your place....Really?! And she said yes?... No, no, I just thought...I can help.... Yes, I'm serious.... Ok. Ok. Take it easy. I'll be right over."

PETERSON HOUSE

****

Claire rushes around trying to tidy up the disheveled house, throwing plastic Lego pieces and toy dinosaurs under cushions and behind plants. She stops to check her look in the mirror, and says with a heavy sigh, "This is good, right? Right?"

Deep breath. In through the nose, out through the mouth. Ok. Ready. Then…"AAARGH!" she steps on a sharp plastic Lego piece.

The doorbell rings. She takes one last deep breath, and the door opens. Danny Muldoon stands on the front porch dressed in a cheesy retro blue tuxedo from the 1980's. In his hand is an enormous bouquet of flowers – literally every flower imaginable. He looks ridiculous.

Muldoon clears his throat. "I, ah, I didn't have intel on your specific flower of choice…so, I requested them all."

"Wow," says Claire struggling to hold the oversized bouquet in her hands. "Well, they certainly are all here, aren't they? You look…um, nice. I like your suit."

"Too much?" he asks.

But Muldoon doesn't need an answer – the look on Claire's face says it all. He angrily mutters, "I'm gonna kill that kid."

"Make yourself at home. I just need to check on dinner," Claire says escorting him in.

Muldoon begins to wander the living room, his fingers brushing past the books lined on shelves and piled high on the floor.

"You guys do a lot of reading, huh?" he says loud enough so Claire can hear him from the kitchen.

"We do," she shouts back. "Molly especially."

"So, ah, where's your TV?" he asks nervously.

"We don't have one," Claire yells back.

Muldoon stops dead in his tracks, petrified. Shit. He reaches into his pocket for a DVD of THE NOTEBOOK, and thinks to himself, 'What the hell am I supposed to do now?'

Claire waltzes back in with two glasses of wine. Muldoon quickly slides the DVD case back into the pocket of his powder blue tuxedo.

"Come. Sit," she instructs him. The three dogs sit on command. So does Muldoon.

He can't think of anything to say, he's dying inside. What a nightmare.

"So, um, no television at all, huh?" he says finally breaking the silence.

"No. Sorry. Did you want to watch something?" Claire asks innocently.

"Well, I thought we could..." he removes the trusty notepad from his breast pocket and reads, "ah, Netflix and chill."

Claire spits her wine.

"But, since you don't have a TV, I guess we can just do the chill part," Muldoon says, oblivious.

"Do you even know what that means?" Claire asks trying not to laugh.

"Yes. Ah, No. No, not at all."

Claire types into her cell phone, then shows Muldoon the real meaning of the 'Netflix and Chill' term. He's mortified.

"I'm gonna kill that kid!" he mumbles through gritted teeth.

Claire smiles. "When Ben was young, he didn't like noise. For a while, we couldn't even have the lights on, so we got rid of the TV. Molly fights me over it, but ... you get used to the quiet. We can just sit and talk."

"Sure. Just talk. Perfect," says Muldoon. It's his worst nightmare. She's combining his Terrifying List Numbers 5 and 6 together They stare ahead in silence.

"This is nice, right? Right?" says Claire, equally uncomfortable.

Suddenly, smoke billows from the kitchen. A fire alarm blares, breaking the silent tension.

MULDOON'S APARTMENT

****

"You have all that video equipment, and you can't even work a microwave?!" Andrew yells at Skype, fanning smoke from the burnt popcorn.

"Don't blame me," says Skype as tries to remove the batteries from a smoke alarm. "That thing is ancient." He's right. The microwave is enormous, and old, like everything else in Muldoon's tired apartment. He hasn't updated a thing since his mother passed away.

Skype heads into the living room and plops onto the worn Lay-Z-Boy recliner. He grabs the remote and begins flipping through channels.

CLICK

"Gawd, I really am a loser," he says aloud.

CLICK

"Saturday night. I'm eating burnt popcorn and watching a movie with a dude."

CLICK

"At least I hooked my boy Muldoon up on his date though, right?"

CLICK

"There's never anything good on."

CLICK

"I'm so bored."

Skype looks towards the adjacent bedroom.

"Yo, let's go see if he's got any 'Cop stuff' in there. You know...like, contraband," he says hopping out of the chair.

"Do you even know what contraband means?" asks Andrew.

"Yes. Ah, No. Not at all, actually," Skype admits. "But let's see if we can find some anyway."

Muldoon's bedroom is military clean, the bed made so tight you could bounce a quarter on it. His mother Marion was a real stickler for tidiness. She certainly wouldn't be happy with empty pizza boxes or empty beer cans her son leaves lying around the apartment.

Andrew is feeling uneasy. "We shouldn't be in here."

132

"Come on. It's bad enough we're in on a Saturday night missing all the parties." Skype spots the cardboard box marked **EVIDENCE** on the closet floor. "Yo! Jackpot!"

"I don't think this is a good idea," says Andrew reluctantly, but Skype is already rifling through the contents. He removes a large envelope and spills an assortment of photographs onto the bed.

Andrew's voice is barely above a whisper. "That's...that's my mom."

He begins to sift through old black and white photos and Polaroids. Vacations at the beach. Trips to the mountains. New York. Rome. Paris. His mother is probably not far from Andrew's age in many of them.

Skype can see that his friend is confused and speaks up. "So, you guys traveled a lot, huh?"

Andrew stares at the photos, perplexed. "No," he says, his words measured and firm. "Actually, we never left the house."

He removes a metal desk plate: **ALLISON HUGHES - MORGAN STANLEY FINANCIAL ADVISORS.**

"She used to work in New York?" asks Skype. "That's cool."

Andrew is momentarily speechless, reeling with each revelation, and meekly replies, "I guess."   His mother never shared anything about her happy, well-traveled life before being stuck in in Somerset.

Skype reaches into the box and finds a thick black ledger.

"That's from the store," Andrew tells him. "My Dad kept notes so he could make personal recommendations for every customer."

"Cool," replies Skype. "Netflix, before Netflix."

"My dad, he knew every movie - all the lines and stuff," continues Andrew staring at the photos, trying to make some sense of it all. "But my mom...well, she's the one who taught me what the lines really meant."

Skype reads the ledger and says, "You gotta be kidding."

"What?" asks Andrew.

"Dude. Best! Find! Ever!" says Skype, his eyes wide with excitement.   But Andrew isn't listening – he's too busy looking at a manila folder he found at the bottom of the box titled: **ALLISON WILDEN**. He scans Muldoon's notes

"Let's go," Andrew says firmly.

"What's in that folder?"

"I said let's go! Now!" he snaps, then angrily throws the folder back into the box.

PETERSON HOUSE

****

Claire stares at the burnt roast smoldering in her sink. All she can do is laugh, pour an oversized glass of wine and head back to the living room to join Muldoon and try to salvage this smoky, disaster of a dinner date.

"I got Ben settled back down. That alarm really upset him. I'm so sorry about that."

"It's fine," Muldoon reassures her.

Claire sits back into the couch, as deep as the cushion will let her, as if hoping she could just sink in and float away. "I had a beautiful dinner planned. I had everything planned," she says with a heavy sigh, more melancholy than angry.

She holds her glass of wine in the air and gives a mock toast. "Ladies and gentlemen, this is your Captain speaking. Welcome to Holland."

Muldoon looks at her confused. Holland?

Claire tries to explain.

"There was this article I read years ago. 'Welcome to Holland.' I think every parent with a special needs kid knows it."

She looks off and recites from memory.

"'When you find out you're going to have a baby, it's like planning a fabulous trip to Italy. You buy a bunch of guide books and make your wonderful plans. The Coliseum. Michelangelo's David. The gondolas in Venice. It's all so exciting. And after months of anticipation, the day finally arrives, so you pack your bags and off you go. But when the plane lands, the pilot comes on and says, 'Welcome to Holland.' What do you mean Holland? I'm supposed to be in Italy. All my life I've dreamed of going to Italy. But there's been a change in the flight plan. You landed in Holland.'"

She picks up a plastic Lego piece from the end table beside her.

"'But they haven't taken you to a horrible, disgusting place, it's - it's just a different place. So, you have to go out and buy new guide books. Learn a new language. Meet a whole new group of people that you would never have met. And after you've been there for a while and you catch your breath, you look around - you begin to notice that Holland has windmills, and Rembrandts and tulips.'"

She reflects and begins to sadly twirl the red plastic Lego between her fingers.

"'But everyone you know is busy coming and going from Italy...and they're all bragging about what a wonderful time they had there. And you say, Yeah, that's where I was supposed to go.'"

Her body language changes from sadness to resolution. She turns to face Muldoon.

"But, if you spend your whole life sad that you didn't get to Italy, you'll never be free to enjoy all the beautiful tulips in Holland, right? Right?"

Muldoon reaches across his lap and takes her hand. "Do you know I've had a crush on you since High School?"

"Really?"

"I think it was your Unicorn notebook," he says with a smirk. "It's just...I never knew how to talk to you. I never knew how to talk to anyone."

Claire smiles and looks him in the eye. "Talking is so over rated."

Muldoon moves in close, about to kiss her when -- "AAARGH!" he yelps in pain and pulls a sharp Lego piece from under his hip.

Ben cries out from his room. Claire looks at Muldoon as if to say, 'Sorry,' then takes off to check on her son.

The moment is lost.

*WELCOME TO HOLLAND by Emily Perl Kingsley. 1987 ©

****

Andrew and Molly share a milkshake with two straws at the local Diner. They look just like Danny Zukko and Sandy Olson in GREASE.

"It's better if we had an old-fashioned ice cream place," Andrew tells her. "But this will do."

Molly smiles. "I've had so much fun on these dates, Andrew. Thank you."

Andrew looks her in the eye, and says, "*'Life moves pretty fast. If you don't stop and look around once in a while, you could miss it'.*"

Molly is mesmerized. "You know, most High School kids, all they ever do is try to be someone else," she tells him. "But not you. You're so unique and original."

Andrew feels a tinge of guilt.

"Tell me about your old school," she asks. "What was it like?"

Andrew squirms in his seat. "Well, um, it was...it was a lot smaller. We only had, like, a few students."

Molly is a bit confused, but so smitten with all things Andrew, she doesn't care. She looks off and wonders aloud, "Maybe it was the kind of school that didn't have rules. Maybe it was the kind of school where people were nice to each other. No Plastics, or Jocks or Freaks and Nerds. Just kids. Just people - people who actually talk with each other. Does a school like that even exist? Do people like that even exist?"

"Maybe in the movies," Andrew answers.

"Maybe. I certainly wouldn't know," she states as a matter of fact.

Bells jingle above the Diner's front doorway. Andrew immediately looks up out of habit.

"Why do you always do that?" Molly asks. "Whenever we're out, you always look up when you hear bells."

She waits. After a moment of searching for an answer, Andrew confesses.

"We had bells like that in our store. Every time someone entered, they would jingle, and I'd look up, thinking it was my mother. But it never was. It was just families, coming and going as they pleased."

There is a real jealousy in his voice. His words turn measured and firm.

"For a while, I really thought she'd come back. I grew to hate the sound of those bells. And then I realized...so did she."

Molly looks at the boy across the table from her. Mature. Confident. Resolved.

The bells jingle again as another customer enters, but this time Andrew jokingly locks his gaze on Molly, trying his best not to look up.

"Yo! Whaddup, guys?"

The special moment is broken when Skype suddenly pops his head between them.

"Oh, hey, Skype," smiles Molly. "You want to join us?"

Andrew drills him with a look. Skype gets the not-so-subtle hint. "No. No, it's cool. I'll just sit over here - leave you two lovebirds alone," he says sliding into the booth behind them.

Molly and Andrew go back to their milkshake.

"Thanks for sharing - about your Mom," Molly tells Andrew and tenderly takes his hand.

142

"My mom...she was really smart.," Andrew tells her. "Home schooled me in everything. Math. Social Studies. Even taught me how to dissect a penguin."

Molly laughs. "Stop that. She did not."

"I mean, my Dad's heart was always in the right place. He was just kind of, I don't know...different. Then after my mother left," he looks away for a moment. "I could tell things weren't right."

Molly can see that he's struggling. She squeezes his hand, gives a knowing, warm smile and says, "'*We're all pretty bizarre. Some of us are just better at hiding it, that's all.*'"

Andrew smiles back, still feeling guilty, so he switches gears to lighten the mood.

"My mom was sweet, but tough, you know? This one time, she took in a homeless teenager from the rough side of the tracks. He couldn't read but was great at football."

"Really?" says Molly, confused but impressed.

"Yeah. She was ...ah, she was a huge football fan," Andrew continues. "And the kid, well, the kid was huge, too. He saved my life one time in a car crash."

Skype is listening from the booth behind them. He slouches down and rolls his eyes.

"That's amazing," says enamored Molly, then notices the clock on the wall. "Oooh, Jeeze. I gotta go."

She leans in, whispers, "You are amazing," then surprises Andrew with a kiss on the cheek.

Andrew beams as he watches Molly hurry off.

Skype slides into her empty seat.   "Homeless youth? Football player? Car crash? You never told me you mother was Sandra Bullock from THE BLIND SIDE. You better make sure Molly never sees that movie."

"It's fine," replies Andrew with a cocky smirk. "I have a better chance of her seeing your YouTube movies. As in, it's never gonna happen."

That stings. Andrew is getting a little *too* cocky.

The bells jingle over the door. Andrew looks up out of habit. It's not his mother. It's Mrs. Johnson, there to pick up the boys.

SOMERSET HIGH SCHOOL

****

Mr. Gleason is in a particularly bad mood. The psoriasis/rosacea/ blood pressure looks much redder than usual. "Find your seats, please. Today!" he commands.

The class rushes to settle in. Ricky bumps into Andrew accidentally/on purpose, spilling his books to the floor as the class giggles. Ricky leans over "Don't forget who runs things around here. You got that, cowboy?"

Skype bends to help his friend retrieve the books. He can sense Andrew's boiling range.

"Let's go Mr. Wilden!" Gleason barks. "Alright, which brilliant young mind handed this in? There's no name on it. You, Miss Standish? Mister Clark? Ah, of course...Mister Sherman."

Ricky sits up from his slouch position, "That's not mine. I didn't..."

"You didn't what, Mister Sherman, read the assignment? That's painfully obvious. Do I need to remind you all of the upcoming mid-term?"

Ricky looks to his Sidekicks with a reassuring smirk, as if to say, 'we got this.'

Mr. Gleason continues his rant. "Is anyone paying attention? It's all right here in the book, people. Just read."

The class is terrified. Molly raises a hand. "I read the book, Mr. Gleason. I thought..."

"You *thought*?" snaps Gleason. "What did you *think,* Miss Peterson?"

Even though Molly is fiercely strong and independent, there's something about Mr. Gleason's mood and tone that makes her nervous. "I...I just thought you'd like a different perspective," she tells him. "Something more...original."

"You were off topic, Miss Peterson," he tells Molly mockingly holding up her paper. "Judgmental. Overly opinionated. The syllabus was created for a reason. Leave the *thinking* to me, will you Miss Peterson? Just stick to the subject matter and give me what I ask for."

Molly's shoulder's slump and she slides deep in her seat, as deep at the chair will let her, as if hoping she could just sink in and float away.

Andrew has seen enough. He gives a loud muffled cough and yells, "'*Eat me.*'"

The class is hushed with silence. Mr. Gleason glares.

"What? Who...who said that?"

A voice replies, "'*You gonna bark all day little doggie...or are you gonna bite?*'"

Mr. Gleason looks ready to explode. "Wilden?!"

Andrew replies, "'*Hey bud, what's your problem?*'"

"Are you out of your mind?!" snaps Gleason with anger and surprise.

Andrew doesn't flinch. He stares directly at the teacher and says, "'*You are a sad strange little man. And you have my pity.*'"

The class is shocked. No one says a thing. Everyone just stares in awe. Molly leans to Andrew and whispers, "Stop. You're going to get in trouble."

He replies calmly, "'*Frankly, my dear, I don't give a damn.*'"

Gleason is homicidal. It's not the rosacea, or the psoriasis - it's his blood pressure from pure anger. "I'm not going to take this from some...some home-schooled *savant.*"

Suddenly, there is the squeal of a chair as Skype bolts up from his seat.

"Sit down Mister Johnson," Gleason tells him. But Skype remains standing, ready to defend his friend.

"Do you have any idea where this 'home school' was, Mr. Gleason?" Skype asks with an air of confidence.

"I said sit down!" Gleason commands – but it's no use, he's lost all control.

"COMING ATTRACTIONS video store. Ever heard of it?" Skype says with a smirk.

Gleason is visibly shaken. The whole class can see it. Skype reaches into his backpack and pulls out Mr. Wilden's thick black ledger.

"Apparently, you were quite a regular back in the day," announces Skype calmly scanning the pages. "Let's see here. Vernon Gleason. Ah, here it is. You rented TITANIC eight times."

"'*I'm so cold Jack,*'" says Andrew in a high pitch voice.

The class giggles. Skype continues to read the ledger. "TWILIGHT. You rented that eleven times."

"'*Hold on tight spider monkey,*'" Andrew mocks.

Nervous laughter fills the room. Skype is loving every minute of this. "Let's see," he continues. "Ah, SISTERHOOD OF THE TRAVELING PANTS. Fifteen rentals."

Howls of laughter. Gleason is reeling.

"And of course," continues Skype, "that wonderful tale of one magical summer in the Catskills – DIRTY DANCING. You rented that a store record thirty-seven times."

The room explodes with laughter. Gleason wants to die. Andrew takes the ledger from Skype and approaches the desk.

"'*Nobody puts baby in a corner...*' Vern," he says and drops the ledger hard onto Gleason's lap.

Skype and Andrew high-five each other and walk out like Kings. For a moment, Molly thinks they resemble Ricky's Sidekicks, high-fiving whenever he does something cool – and she's not sure what to make of this newfound air of confidence.

Skype turns to the class before heading out the door and says with a cocky grin, *"'There's a new Sherriff in town. Ya'll be cool.'"*

In the back of the room, Ricky Sherman is as angry, red and homicidal as Vern Gleason.

PETERSON HOUSE

****

"Hey guys," says Claire as she bends to greet the dogs. She calls to the other room. "I had to come home to get something. Has anyone seen a folder on Andrew Wilden? Mom? Hello?"

No response. She peeks into Ben's play room full of Legos and plastic dinosaurs. Empty. 'That's odd,' she thinks, and heads upstairs to Molly's room.

"Molly, where's your brother?" she asks peaking her head in.

"I just got home," she replies, reading at her desk. "Isn't he with Nana May?"

A sudden rush of panic floods Claire's face. She hurries down to the kitchen.

"Mom, where's Ben? Mom?"

Nana May sits meditating, surrounded by candles. She can't hear over the loud Joni Mitchell music.

Claire yells out, "Mom?!"

Nana May snaps out of her deep meditative trance.

"What...? Why are you home so early?"

"Where is Ben, Mom?" Claire asks, trying to control her panic.

"Don't be mad," Nana May replies sheepishly.

"Where is he?" Claire insists.

After a moment, Nana May finally admits. "He's...he's with Danny Muldoon. At his apartment."

Claire is visibly shaken. "What?! Why?"

"Claire, stop. Let me explain," Nana May pleads.

But Claire is already out the door.

MULDOON'S APARTMENT

****

"Where is Ben?" yells Claire almost hysterical as she barges past Muldoon into his apartment.

"Claire? I...I can explain," he says, but Claire will have none of it.

"You have no right to take my son."

"I...I thought it might be good for him to get out," Muldoon replies, trying his best to calm the situation.

"You thought?!" snaps Claire, her eyes filled with rage.

"Will you just let me talk for a second?" says Muldoon attempting to calm her. The firmness of his tone finally makes Claire stop. She takes a deep breath, allowing him a moment to explain.

"Ok. Now, just listen. Couple weeks ago, I went by your house to pick up Andrew - I was taking him to Lincoln Park since I figured he's never been. Well, Andrew wasn't there, and your Mom asked if I'd take Ben."

"She what?!" snaps Claire.

"I know, I know…but your mom said Ben had never been there either." He pauses knowing, the next words may hurt. "She said he'd never been anywhere, actually."

Claire just bites her lip.

"We came back to my place to get Andrew, and he's here watching a movie on TV. I can't remember what it was, all I know is Ben's face lights up. He's drawn to it. Laughing. Repeating the lines. I couldn't get him to budge."

Claire looks at Ben sitting quietly. He seems calm, not stemming. He's just contently watching the animated Disney movie playing on the television.

Muldoon speaks up. "We've been coming back just about every afternoon. You said he needs a routine." He pauses, and with his words measured and deliberate says, "It's not good for anyone to live a lonely, socially isolated life."

The words sit out there and float around, as if they're looking for someone to land on. Andrew. Skype. Claire. Ben. Molly. Muldoon. They're all just trying to fit in – trying to belong to something or someone.

Claire is still trying to wrap her head around it all.

"I'm sorry," says Muldoon. "I should have told you. I just thought it might be good because…"

"Because, why?" she snaps, her voice cracking. "Because he's so unhappy? Because he has a bad mother? Because…"

"Because he needs to leave the house!" says a voice from across the room. They turn to see Andrew, the sternness taking them both by surprise.

"My father thought he was doing the right thing, keeping us safe in his own little world. In the end, all he did was tear us apart."

Andrew looks to Ben, then back to Claire. "You need to let him find his way. You need to let him be part of the world."

Then, a voice just above a whisper says, "Just like Ariel."

It's Ben.

Claire turns, stunned, as if a lightning bolt has gone through the room. It's the first time she's heard her son say anything in years.

"What? Did…did you say something, Ben?"

"Just like Ariel," Ben repeats, his eyes never leaving THE LITTLE MERMAID playing on the TV screen.

Claire's head is spinning. She looks at Ben with disbelief, then turns to Muldoon for answers. "I...I don't understand."

Muldoon does his best to explain. "I read about this family in Boston. They have a son just like Ben who stopped talking when he was about three. He started watching Disney films and would act out the characters. But he didn't just mimic them, he seemed to understand and relate to their emotions. So, the family started speaking to him in the character's voice. And it worked. He eventually came out of his shell - and they found a way to communicate again."

"I...I don't know what to say," she says, her lip trembling and her eyes flooded with tears

"It was all Andrew's idea," Muldoon tells her.

She kneels beside Ben as he continues to silently watch the movie, gently rocking back and forth. He seems different. Content. Happy.

Claire hugs her son - and he lets her.

SOMERSET HIGH SCHOOL

****

Skype and Andrew stand by their lockers as the three Plastics saunter on down the hallway.

"Hey guys," says Plastic 1. Skype and Andrew do a double-take to make sure she is in fact speaking to them.

"We heard about what happened the other day in Mr. Gleason's class," adds Plastic 2. "Super cool."

"We're having a party Saturday night," Plastic 3 tells them. "You guys should come."

Skype almost shits himself. "Us guys? Like, him and me? Really? "

"Yeah. Sure," replies Plastic 1, granting his wish like a Queen from her throne. The Plastics go back to their important iPhone texting, and saunter away down the hall.

"Did that just happen?" Skype asks "Did we just get invited to a party? A *High School* party? I've lived in this town fifteen years and have never been invited to anything! Cameron Broderick's pool party. Jake Schoeffling's Bar Mitzvah. Nancy Ringwald's birthday party at Applebee's - although everyone got food poisoning, so, yep, kinda glad I missed that one. But, Holy Shit, bro, we're going to a party! With girls and beer and girls and a keg and girls!" He talks himself down. "Ok. Be cool, bro. Be cool. Nice job, brother," and gives Andrew a rousing high five.

"*You can be my wing man anytime,*" smirks Andrew.

Skype smiles back. "*You can be mine.*"

Andrew spins the combination on his locker - and it opens with ease. He's finally getting the hang of things around here. He smiles and closes the locker door to see --- Mr. Gleason, red-faced and furious, standing on the other side.

"Mister Wilden," says Gleason with an ominous tone. "They'd like to see you in the Principal Shepherd's office. Now."

****

The waiting area outside Principal Shepherd's office is drab and cold. Shelves are filled with three-ring binders. The computer screens have yellow sticky notes attached along the bottom to remind the underpaid Secretary to order more supplies. Andrew can see that she looks miserable in her job.

On the wall are three framed posters of beautiful landscapes; A snowy mountaintop. A rolling, deep blue ocean.

158

A beautiful, glowing sunset. Below each picture in large bold font are words: **MOTIVATION. CHALLENGE. PERSISTENCE**.

Clearly, they are intended to inspire young minds as they sit outside the Principal's office awaiting their fate.

Andrew stares up at the posters. He's pretty sure he's gonna see these exact same ones hanging over some cubicle or office lunch room for the next 30 or 40 years. They'll be more appropriate when he's saddled with a mortgage and college loans and car payments and hates his job like the underappreciated Secretary that was just ordered to the auditorium to bring extra paper clips, or the overworked Janitor cleaning the diarrhea explosion in the men's room stall that Andrew passed on his way to the Principal's office.

He thinks to himself, 'Can't I just enjoy being a normal teenager for a little while? Finally? Why does it have to be so hard?'

Andrew used to dream of walking the halls of High School, laughing in lunch lines, hanging by lockers. He's seen every Coming of Age-teenage angst movie about the High School experience from REBEL WITHOUT A CAUSE in the 1950's to MEAN GIRLS over sixty years later. The story never changes. Popular kids make the rules. Unpopular kids need to follow them. He gets it. High School sucks. Being a teenager sucks. But not to Andrew Wilden. He's finally getting his chance.

In the short time he's been at Somerset High, Andrew has already seen the pressure.   College applications. GPA numbers. SAT scores. Sports teams. Fashion choices. Popularity. The Plastics. The Jocks. The Basket cases. The Nerds. Andrew wanted to experience everything. But most of all, he wanted those quiet moments of sitting around and talking and making profound connections. Maybe even make one or two friendships that will matter and last. Isn't that what being a teenager is all about? Isn't that what *life* is all about?

Andrew grabs a nearby Sharpie pen and draws a thick black line through the words **MOTIVATION CHALLENGE PERSISTENCE** and scribbles in their place **SMILE RELAX ENJOY.**

He sits back, pleased with himself and his new Super Cool status at Somerset High. But the feeling is short lived. The door to Principal Shepherd's office opens. Claire Peterson is in there. There's a quiet tension and seriousness in the room as he enters.

"I'm sorry," Andrew begins. "I...I can explain. Mr. Gleason was..."

"This isn't about what happened in Mr. Gleason's room, Andrew," states Principal Shepherd. He turns to Claire for her help. She finally looks up from her lap.

"There's been a change, Andrew," she says with a sad, formal tone, finding it hard to make eye contact. "A house just opened up in Fall River and..."

"Is this because of Ben?" he interrupts. "I was only trying to help."

"No, Andrew, I know. What you did...I...I could never begin to thank you. But there are rules, protocol, and, well, this woman in Fall River is certified."

Andrew can feel his whole body tense.

"Did Molly and Skype know about this?" he asks.

Claire's shoulders slump. "I'm really sorry. It was only temporary."

The word hits Andrew like a hammer. Temporary. Like a rental - one of the video cassettes from his father's store, passed from house to house, exchanged between families and friends, but never staying in one place for too long.

In that moment, Andrew realizes he's going to be moved - and he gets angry.

SOMERSET HIGH SCHOOL

****

The Plastics sit at their table in the cafeteria, heads down on their cell phones texting. Nothing changes. Ever.

"Guys, my mom made me watch this wicked old movie the other night. I thought I'd hate it, but - check this guy in it. He is super cute," says Plastic 1 turning her screen to show the others.

"Oh, my Gawd," screeches Plastic 2. "This is, like, my mom's favorite movie."

Plastic 3 agrees. "I've seen this. Totally awesome."

Molly is at the table behind them, quietly reading, but can't help but overhear the conversation.

"Ooh, this is, like, my favorite part," says Plastic 1 turning up the volume. Words flow out from the tiny speaker. "'*Life moves pretty fast. If you don't stop and look around once in a while, you could miss it.*'"

The look on Molly's face says it all. Surprise. Confusion.

"Guys. Saturday's party. We should make it, like, an 80's theme," says Plastic 2.

"Totally," replies Plastic 3. "My mom has cool costume jewelry. We could do all neon and, like, super old music."

Molly is standing behind them, staring at the screen of their iPhone.

"I know this," she says with a puzzled look.

"You?" asks Plastic 1. "You've seen this movie?"

"I thought you didn't have a TV," adds Plastic 3.

Molly keeps staring at the phone. "We don't. But I...I heard that somewhere."

The Plastics look at each other knowingly and giggle. "Maybe she should ask her boyfriend. He's seen, like, every movie ever."

They laugh among themselves. Plastic 1 scribbles something on a piece of paper and hands it to Molly.

"Here," she says with a sly smirk. "Google this."

Molly walks away in total confusion, staring at the note in her hand.

MULDOON'S APARTMENT

****

The bedroom is thick with tension as Andrew packs his duffle bag.

"So, ah, you sure you got everything?" asks Muldoon trying help.

No response.

"Claire said this lady is really nice."

"You don't have to do this," Andrew firmly replies.

"Do what?" asks Muldoon.

"Pretend like you care," he snaps, the anger and hurt in his voice hitting Muldoon like a punch. "I found that box in your room," Andrew tells him. "I saw the report. A manila folder with her name on it? It said you left my mom a ton of messages."

Muldoon reacts hard to the discovery. He doesn't know how to respond.

"I...I was going to tell you, but..." Muldoon stops. He knows he needs to tell Andrew the truth. "Yes, Andrew. We did locate the subject. Mrs. Wilden. I mean, your mother. She has yet to respond. I'm sorry."

Muldoon's cell phone buzzes. It's Claire. He ignores it.

Andrew finishes packing his duffel bag. "Here, I don't need this," he says tossing a Red Sox cap from their happy night at Fenway Park onto the bed. "I don't need anything."

Muldoon stands alone in the room, angry, confused and sad. He reaches into his back pocket for a glossy pamphlet and stares at an application for **Massachusetts Foster Care.** He tosses it onto the bed where it falls beside the Red Sox hat.

His cell phone buzzes again. It's Claire. He ignores.

FALL RIVER, MA

****

Andrew and Claire stand on the front steps of a drab, sad house, the duffle bag of clothes hanging over his shoulder. The odor of cigarettes and kitty litter wafts in the air.

"This will be good, right? Right? Fall River High, home of the Pirates. Aaarrrgh!" says Claire trying to make the best of it.

Andrew is having none of what she's selling.

The door opens and Mrs. O'Hara, a plain, older woman who seems nice enough greets them. "You must be Andrew. So nice to meet you."

Andrew says nothing. He doesn't even look up. Claire steps in to help. "I'm Claire Peterson. We spoke on the phone."

"Yes. Of course," says Mrs. O'Hara escorting them in. The house is as tired inside as it is outside, only, the odor of cigarettes and kitty litter is stronger. Claire attempts to put on a brave face. "This is nice. Isn't this nice Andrew?"

Silence.

This is her cue to leave. She turns to Mrs. O'Hara. "Well, um...we can finalize all the paperwork Monday."

167

Claire peaks back through the window at Andrew. To her, he looks like a little boy - overwhelmed, lonely, sad, but mostly... angry.

****

Andrew scans his new room. There's a bed. Nightstand. On top of a worn brown oak dresser is an old Zenith TV with a rabbit ear antenna.

"Not sure if it works, but you can feel free to try," says Mrs. O'Hara trying to help. "Well, I'll let you get settled in."

Andrew drops his duffle bag in the corner and sits on the edge of the bed. He reaches into his pocket for the black remote control that belonged to his father and aims it at the old Zenith. It doesn't work. Of course, it doesn't. Nothing works!

Things used to work, though - before. Before his mother left. Before his father had a breakdown. Before everything in his life changed. Before he was nothing but a problem.

He slides the remote back into his pocket, opens the bedroom window, and runs off into the night.

CHAPTER III

PETERSON HOUSE

****

It's been a long day and Claire is emotionally exhausted. Moving Andrew has taken its toll. She quietly enters Ben's room to check on her sleeping son. Walking gingerly in her bare feet, she steps on the sharp edge of Lego piece, and muffles a scream. MMMmnpphhaaargh!

Perfect. Just perfect.

"How you doin', Ben?" she whispers, talking more to herself than her son. "Did you have a good day? I had a tough one. We had to relocate Andrew. He's not talking to me. Danny's not talking to me. Molly won't talk to me until we get a television. And you? Well, we're working on it, right? Right?"

She gives a sad smile.

"Anything you wanna talk about? I don't know, like, maybe, how you secretly hate Legos? How these little plastic pieces of pain seem to always find the bottom of my feet?"

She twirls the Lego piece between her fingers.

"How you look everywhere, trying to pick up the pieces, but there's always one you missed...and how you just can't seem to get your life organized."

Ben whispers from his slumber, *"Just keep swimming."*

Claire looks at her son. "Did you say something?"

He repeats the words, almost singing. *"'Just keep swimming. Just keep swimming. Just keep swimming, swimming, swimming.'"*

Claire smiles, and whispers, "I will, buddy. I will. Goodnight."

****

Claire leans with her back to the kitchen sink and stares at the empty screen on her cell phone.

"Have you heard from Danny yet?" Nana May asks her tired daughter.

"No. He's pretty upset," she replies. "I did tell him the Andrew living situation was only temporary, but..."

"Why don't you go over and talk to him," Nana May says softly, trying to help.

"I'll just send another text," replies Claire thinking some dreamy spiritual lecture from her Hippie Mom is the last thing she needs right now.

"Why not use a carrier pigeon, it's just as personal?" snaps her mother forcefully. "Now, come and sit. I said, sit!"

For the first time, all three dogs listen to her and sit! So does Claire. Nana May joins her daughter at the kitchen table.

"This generation with your texting and your phones. We've been all the way to the moon but struggle to start a conversation with the person across from us," she says grabbing Claire's cell phone to emphasize her point.

"This same technology that brings us close to people far away, takes us far away from people that are actually close."

She looks Claire in the eye. "Pause. Reset. Reflect. Take a moment to become more conscious, more aware."

Claire thinks on that for a moment. "That's pretty good, Mom. Joni Mitchell?"

"Naw," says Nana May with a sheepish grin. "I saw it on YouTube."

They both bust out laughing at the irony.

SOMERSET, MA

****

Saturday night in Somerset. Young kids play video games, couples settle in to download movies, and High School kids sneak in to party at the vacant home of any friend whose parents are on Cape Cod for the weekend.

This weekend, it's at the home of Plastic 1. The house is wildly overcrowded. Loud music plays on the stereo. Cheap beer is poured from a 'fake ID-obtained' keg into red Solo cups. The whole place is decorated as if they stepped back in time to the 1980's. Everyone is dressed all Gnarly and Rad and, like, Totally Bitchin'. Girls wear huge bright neon earrings, side pony tails and fanny packs. Guys wear stone washed jeans, bomber jackets and Miami Vice linen slacks.

Skype strolls into the party trying to contain his excitement and do his best to be cool. He's dressed like Duckie from PRETTY IN PINK; a blazer covered in band pins, round sunglasses, a Bolo tie, and a hip little-old-man hat. His face lights up when he sees Andrew standing by the keg.

"Yo, Wing man! I thought you were in Fall River. How'd you get back here?"

Andrew ignores him and downs a Solo cup full of beer.

"What are you mad at me for?" Skype asks him.

"You coulda' just told me you didn't want me around," snaps Andrew pouring himself another beer from the tap.

"I didn't know anything about..." Skype begins to explain, but Andrew isn't listening. He downs the beer.

The Plastics approach the keg dressed as 80's icons Madonna, Cyndi Lauper, and Pat Benatar.

Plastic 1 (Madonna) yells to the crowd, "Andrew, tell these guys what you said to Mr. Gleason."

"It was so awesome," giggles Plastic 2 (Cyndi Lauper).

Andrew is loving his new-found celebrity and repeats a line he used on Gleason. "'*You are a sad strange little man, and you have my pity.*'"

Someone shouts, "Yeah! Buzz Lightyear, dude! '*To infinity and beyond!*'" and hands Andrew a full cup from the keg.

They all begin to chant, "Buzz! Buzz! Buzz! Buzz!"

Andrew downs the beer, slams the cup to the ground and screams, "'*Aaaarrrrrggghh! Kelly Clarkson!*'"

The crowd erupts in cheers. Skype is getting concerned. He leans to his friend and whispers, "Whoa. Take it easy, Andrew."

Andrew looks at Skype, his eyes getting blurry, and slurs, "*Grab a drink, don't cost nothin'.*"

Skype tries to intervene. "Dude, stop. You're drunk."

But Andrew isn't listening. He drapes a condescending arm around Skype's neck and says, "*Bring me a pitcher of beer every seven minutes until somebody passes out. Then bring one every 10 minutes.*"

Andrew shouts, *"We're goin' streakin' in the quad!"*

The crowd loves it. "Yeah!! Woo Hoo!"

Andrew jumps onto a chair, raises his arms to the sky and screams, "*I am a Golden God!*"

The party erupts in cheers. It's official - Andrew is the coolest kid at the party. Maybe the coolest kid at Somerset High.

Ricky Sherman watches the performance from across the room – and now he's really pissed off.

Skype meanders through the cheering crowd, pulls out his cell phone and starts to text.

PETERSON HOUSE

****

Molly has her nose in a book, alone on Saturday night.   She used to have friends - lots of friends, in grade school. They'd sit and talk and laugh and comb each other's hair and have play dates and dance parties. Then the internet came along and suddenly all her friends were in chat rooms and had AIM screennames. They didn't sit and talk anymore - they'd just send each other messages.

That's about the same time Ben started having problems at school and at home. He hated light, and noise - any kind of noise - so Molly and Claire had to speak in hushed tones and turn off anything electronic. They never consciously made the decision to get rid of computers and TV, it was just that they never turned them on. And eventually, the television in the living room became just another piece of furniture. When Claire decided to move home from Baltimore to Somerset, taking the television along wasn't even an option. Eventually, not having a TV in the house became the new normal - whatever normal means.

Molly found her escape in books, and after a while she put up a wall, a kind of hard exterior to shelter herself from the outside world. They can keep their Pop Culture and Social Media and Instagram influencers. Fiercely independent Molly forced herself _not_ to watch their stupid reality TV shows and download their immature internet videos. She wore it like a badge of honor. She was not about to become just another Cookie Cutter Plastic.

Maybe High School would be different, she thought. A fresh start. Maybe her friends that used to sit and talk with her would sit and talk with her again. Maybe if her mother let them have a TV, she could sit at the cafeteria table near the bathrooms and talk about the latest shows.

But High School wasn't different. It was just more of the same. And Molly _liked_ being different. Well...sometimes. Sometimes it might be nice to have a TV and be part of the conversation – but she would never admit that to The Plastics.

The glow of her mother's work laptop fills the room. The scribbled piece of paper given to her by the Plastics sits beside the keyboard. Molly types into the search bar: TOP ROMANTIC MOVIE SCENES.

With each click of the mouse, her face shows more disappointment. SIXTEEN CANDLES. SAY ANYTHING. THE

NOTEBOOK. Molly is slowly realizing all of her 'original' dates with Andrew were stolen ideas.

She types into the search bar again. A scene from THE BREAKFAST CLUB plays. Emilio Esteves turns to Molly Ringwald and says, "'*I mean, we're all pretty bizarre. Some of us are just better at hiding it, that's all.*'"

Molly looks like she's been punched in the gut.

Her cell phone buzzes.

****

Molly makes her way through the crowded party. She's the only one not dressed in an 80's outfit. Always the outcast.

She finally reaches Skype. "I came as soon as I got your text. What's up with him?"

"I don't know," Skype tells her. "He's a mess."

Andrew spots Molly from across the kitchen. His speech slurred from the alcohol, he yells, "Hey, Mollyssshere. Look everybody. Iss' Molly!"

Molly forces her way through the kitchen and grabs him by the arm. "Andrew, I think it's time to go home."

"Surrre," smiles Andrew. "Good idea. Home. I'm off to your house." He takes a few steps, then stops. "But wait. It's only temporary. Like, a rental, right?"

Molly can see a change in him. Something is wrong. Andrew turns bitter and pulls his arm away. "No, wait. I'm not going to your house. You don't even have a TV."

The crowd laughs. Skype steps in to help. "Come on, Andrew. Let's go."

Andrew looks up. "Oops, sorry Molly, guess I'm going to Skype's house now. Why not, right? Nobody else wants me. At least he has a TV. Huuuuge one, too. Only, he doesn't have anybody to watch it with him."

Skype is stung. He whispers, "Why are you doing this?"

Andrew continues his drunken rant. "Hey, I know! We can go to your house and watch your computer. Show me all your funny little videos. Just me and you, cuz nobody's evah gonna see them, are they? Cuz you're too scared."

The words hit Skype hard. He looks at Andrew and snaps, "You know what? Screw you!"

"Go ahead. Go home," Andrew yells after him, his voice a mixture of jealousy and anger and hurt. "Home to your big TV and your movies...and your perfect family."

Even drunk, Andrew realizes he's gone too far - but it's too late - Skype is gone.

Molly tugs hard at Andrew's arm, spinning him so she can look him directly in the eye. "All this time I thought you were smart and funny and original. Turns out you've just been hiding behind movies. Who's really the scared one?"

Molly's words hit their intended target. She storms out, leaving Andrew alone in the crowded party - friendless.

JOHNSON HOUSE

****

Skype storms into his Man Cave, angry and hurt, his eyes red from crying. He opens the closet, grabs a handful of VHS tapes and DVDs and angrily tosses them across the room. He falls deep into the beanbag chair as tears stream down his cheeks.

The front doorbell rings. Skype can hear muffled voices, then steps approaching. The Man Cave door swings open. Mrs. Johnson and Officer Muldoon are standing in the doorway. There's someone behind them, but Skype doesn't recognize who they are - he's too mad to look closer, and too upset to care.

"Michael," asks Mrs. Johnson. "Do you know where Andrew is?"

"Well, he's not here!" he snaps trying to mask the hurt and anger.

"Watch your tone, young man," his mother scolds.

Skype sits up and collects himself. "Sorry. What...what's this all about?" he asks, his eyes turning to the mysterious person skulking in the doorway.

Muldoon steps aside to reveal a woman in her forties.

"Skype," he says. "This is Allison Wilden. Andrew's mother."

SOMERSET, MA

****

Andrew stumbles down Main Street, past the local Diner, the convenience store, the pizza place. He finally stops in front of the empty shingled video store that was once his home. He reaches into his pocket and removes the black remote control. CRASH! He slams it through the COMING ATTRACTIONS sign stenciled on the front window.

Suddenly, there's a screech of tires. Arms grab Andrew and throw him into the back-seat. The car shifts into gear and speeds off.

****

Ricky and the Sidekicks surround Andrew against the railing that overlooks Somerset. Andrew surveys his situation and says to the threatening clan, "'*The first rule of Fight Club is: You do not talk about Fight Club.*'"

"What is this kid's deal?" asks Ricky, his fists clenched tight.

Andrew looks at him and says, "'*Say 'what' again. I dare you. I double dare you.*'"

He lengthens his body, arms high, one leg out in a Karate Kid crane move, and says, "'*If done right...can no defense.*'"

Ricky looks to the Sidekicks. "What the hell is this kid doing?"

"It's just lines from movies, dude," says a Sidekick. "That's all he ever does."

Drunk Andrew leans forward and whispers, "'*There are a lot of things about me you don't know anything about. Things you wouldn't understand. Things you couldn't understand. Things you shouldn't understand.*'"

Ricky steps close and says with menacing confidence, "Oh, but I do. I saw your file. Never went to school. Never even left that shitty little video store. And your parents? Oh, I know...maybe I should just quote a movie. '*Mother? Mother, where are you?*'"

A Sidekick whispers aloud, "Awe, harsh dude. Is that Bambi?"

"And your old man?" snarls Ricky almost nose to nose with Andrew. "He's batshit crazy."

Andrew swings, but the punch misses wildly. The Sidekicks grab his arms. Andrew struggles to break free, but it's no use.

"You think you can come to my school and be the...what did you call it, *Golden God*?" says Ricky grabbing Andrew by the collar. "That ain't how the pecking order works. Oh, and I looked up Barry Manilow on line. You're dead."

Ricky cocks his arm back. Andrew looks off and says, *"'Toto - I have a feeling we're not in Kansas anymore.'"*

And everything goes dark.

PETERSON HOUSE

****

Claire sits curled on the couch with a book. She looks up when Molly comes through the front door.

"Another adventurous date with Andrew?" she asks.

"I don't think we'll be going on any more adventures for a while," Molly replies sadly, then snuggles her head on her mother's shoulder.

Claire soaks in the quiet moment. "You used to fit right in here, curled up in the triangle of my leg. Remember? This is nice, right? Right?"

"I remember," says Molly, wishing she were little again.

"You'll be off to college soon."

"In two years, Mom."

"I know, but still."

Molly sinks her head deeper into her mother's shoulder, and asks, "Why are boys so complicated."

Claire waits a moment before responding because she really doesn't have an answer. "I don't know, sweetie," she sighs. "I hate to tell you, but it doesn't get any easier when they become men."

"Everything he's been telling me is a lie," Molly admits.

Claire thinks for a bit, then looks straight at her daughter - not preaching, not lecturing — it's just that the words are meant for them both. "You know, sometimes people hide because they're afraid. The world can be really scary."

Molly wipes at a tear. Claire can tell her daughter is hurting, but she's not sure how to help or fix it, she just says plainly, "Andrew sure has been nice to your brother."

Molly lets it all sink in.

Claire looks around the living room. "You think maybe we should get a TV?"

Molly is enjoying the quiet moment with her Mom.

"Naw. I think we'll be fine without one."

"I think we'll be fine too," says Claire kissing her daughter tenderly on the forehead.

Molly hugs her tight.

"Goodnight, Mom."

"Goodnight, sweetheart."

Claire smiles proudly as she watches her mature, fiercely independent, and now heartbroken teenage daughter head upstairs.

A cell phone buzzes.

"Danny? Listen, I am so sorry..."

 Her face falls. "What? But I thought he was at O'Hara's?... I'll be right there."

She grabs her car keys and rushes out.

JOHNSON HOUSE

****

Andrew wakes up, blinking through a groggy head, unsure where he is. A room is filled with DVD cases and VHS cassettes. For a moment Andrew thinks he's back home. Maybe this was all a dream. Yeah, that's it. Like they do with flashbacks and dream sequences in the movies.

A woman wipes his forehead. In his fog, Andrew whispers, "Mom?"

Slowly, things come into focus. He's in Skype's Man Cave with Mrs. Johnson at his bedside.

"Sorry," Andrew tells her. "I...I thought you were someone else."

Mrs. Johnson gives him a caring, reassuring smile and tenderly touches his face. "Everything is going to be OK, Honey. I'll get you more ice."

A figure emerges. Andrew can't make out who it is. The figure approaches slowly, tentatively, until finally, there, standing in the doorway is Allison Wilden. She motions towards the   bed but stops. She can't find words. It's uncomfortable.

"I heard about your father. I came as soon as I..."

"Really?" snaps Andrew, not letting her finish and looking away. "The police said they left you a bunch of messages."

Allison tries to answer. "I was in Europe and..."

"Europe," Andrew snaps again, not masking his bitterness. "Must be nice." The anger in his voice is palpable.

"It was a business trip," she explains. "I work in Manhattan and..."

But Andrew isn't listening. Allison looks down at the floor. "I wanted so many times to come see you, Andrew. I would sit at the train station for hours, trying to decide, but..."

There is no excuse. Allison Wilden knows that, but she tries anyway. "Your father, he has a big heart, but he's...different, you understand that now. I'm glad he's getting help. And you two were so close. You had your movies. Your banter. Sometimes I felt like I didn't belong, you know?"

Andrew can tell she's hurting. He also knows what it feels like not to belong.

Allison looks at her son.

"I know it was wrong, Andrew...but I needed to show you that you could leave too."

They both sit in silence for a moment. Allison is hoping her words are getting through. "Do you remember what I used to whisper in your ear?"

Andrew replies simply, "Every day."

"Life isn't like in the movies. You need to write your own ending."

Andrew touches his swollen black eye, and says, "Yeah, I'm finding that out."

He finally looks up and scans the woman in front of him. His mother has aged a bit since the last time he saw her. She looks softer, more professional, but there's something else about her – Andrew can see it in her eyes and the way she carries herself. That tightly coiled sense of discontentment is gone. His mother is different. She seems content, like she finally is comfortable in her own skin. She belongs to something.

Allison looks proudly at her teenage son, so grown and handsome and mature. "I hoped someday you would understand."

That realization eases some of the tension in the room as they both find a sad smile.

Mrs. Johnson returns with an ice pack to place on Andrew's eye. Allison steps back and watches as she tenderly cares for Andrew. It's the kind of nurturing Allison Wilden never gave her own son, and she suddenly feels out of place.

"I should go," she admits softly.

Andrew watches his mother turn and walk away, only this time he calls out.

"Mom?"

She stops.

"I hear NYU has a really good film school. Maybe I can come check it out."

"I'd like that," Allison tells him, the tears glistening in her eyes. "I'd like that a lot."

And then Allison Wilden hugs her son tight, tighter than ever, as if holding him close could erase the years of loneliness and abandonment.

Mrs. Johnson escorts Allison Wilden out, just as Skype peaks his head in from behind the door.

"Hey," he says meekly.

"Hey."

"So, my mom made this for you," he says handing Andrew a plate of dry white toast. Andrew smiles.

"I was a real jerk last night," he admits.

"Yep. You sure were," agrees Skype. He waits, then, "You were right, though. I should put myself out there. So, you moving to New York now?"

"I don't know. Got school in Fall River Monday," he says and gives a sad, fake cheer, "Go Pirates. Aargh."

"Well, make sure someone shows you around. Like, where the cool kids sit and stuff. You're gonna want the right crew, ya know?" says Skype trying to make the best of it. "At least you won't have to deal with Ricky and the Dumb Dumbs anymore."

They both sit in silence, totally bummed.

Andrew props himself up on the bed and scans The Man Cave filled with VHS tapes, DVDs, audio/video equipment and cameras.

"So, Wing man, let me ask you a question," he says. "You know how to work any of this stuff?"

The friends look at each other. Their eyes suddenly widen as an idea forms - and they begin to hatch a plan.

SOMERSET HIGH SCHOOL

****

Monday at Somerset High. Kids walk the halls, heads down, earplugs in. The flat screen television monitors scroll the morning announcements - but no one is paying attention, they are all too busy texting on their phones.

Suddenly, the screech of microphone feedback is heard over the school PA system. It's deafening - so loud that the kids actually stop what they're doing and listen.

A voice rings out over the loudspeakers, *"Gooooood Mooooorning Red Raiders!"*

The TV monitors hanging in the hallways begin to flicker and scramble. The haunting theme from THE TWILIGHT ZONE plays. Suddenly, Skype appears on screen dressed as Rod Serling. His hair is slicked with Brylcream and he's wearing a dark suit with a thin black tie.

Skype/Rod Serling speaks directly into the camera.

"Submitted for your approval. I give you the High School Athlete."

An image of Ricky Sherman pops onto screens all over school.

"He's popular. Admired. Feared. But he peaks at sixteen. Suddenly, a blown knee. It's rehab. Low SAT scores. Then, it's off to Community College, and before you know it, he's living in Mom's basement with a comb-over, a Dad bod, and he's mowing our lawns."

A photoshopped rendition of middle-aged Ricky Sherman appears on screen. He has a beer belly, dramatic wispy comb-over and a green landscaper jumpsuit. All over school, kids stand and watch the TV monitors giggling with delight.

Ricky's voice is heard over the PA system and echoes through the halls. "See, I got a system here – a pecking order if you will. The Nerds do the work for me, and I let them survive High School. Fair trade if you ask me."

Skype's voice narrates, "It all started in 7th grade..."

Middle school Ricky Sherman appears on the TV monitors. A video clip shows Ricky leaning over, blatantly cheating off a classmate's paper. Young Ricky looks back at the camera, suspicious that someone was watching. Someone was - it was all captured by Skype on his computer when he was home sick.

Skype continues as Rod Serling. "...and it hasn't changed much today."

A series of video clips begin to play on the monitors, all taken from Skype's cell phone; Ricky bullying kids. Ricky cheating off papers. Ricky sneaking into Mr. Gleason's classroom and taking a snapshot of the mid-term exam.

Skype's narrates. "How many times have we been taken advantage of? Made to sit in the front of the classroom, and the back of the cafeteria?!"

Everyone in the school is listening. In the cafeteria, a geeky nerd sits alone in the back. In the hallway, the underappreciated Janitor leans on his broom. In the office, the overworked Secretary listens intently.

On the TV monitors, Skype is now dressed as the President of the United States in a sharp suit and red tie. He stands at a podium and declares, *"'We are fighting for our right to live. To exist. We will not go quietly into the night! We will not vanish without a fight! We're going to live on! We're going to survive! Today we celebrate our Independence Day!'"*

Applause rings throughout the halls.

In quick succession, the TV monitors show scenes of famous bullies getting their just rewards:

Ralphie pummels Scut Farkus in A CHRISTMAS STORY.

The carload of O'Doyle boys drive over a cliff in BILLY MADISON.

Johnny Lawrence is kicked in the face by Daniel in THE KARATE KID.

Regina George gets hit by a bus in MEAN GIRLS.

Marty McFly knocks out Biff Tannen in BACK TO THE FUTURE.

Skype now appears on screen dressed as William Wallace from BRAVEHEART; long straggly hair and his face painted blue. He butchers a Scottish accent. *"Would you be willin' to trade ALL the days, for one chance, just one chance, to tell our enemies that they may take our homework...but they'll never take...OUR FREEDOM!'"*

Cheers echo through the halls of Somerset High and ring throughout the parking lot.

Finally, Skype appears on the screen as himself. He looks directly into the camera and speaks passionately and with purpose.

"The question isn't who is going to let me; it's who is going to stop me."

The forgotten people of the school rise up! The geeky Nerd in the cafeteria dumps milk on a Jock. An overweight girl body slams Plastics 1, 2, and 3 into their locker. The overworked Secretary in the office dumps folders into the trash. The meek, underappreciated Janitor tosses his mop to the floor.

Ricky Sherman is a mess. He is running frantically through the halls trying to turn television monitors off – but it's no use. He jumps up to reach one, misses, and lands face to face with Principal Shepherd. Busted.

CORRIGAN MENTAL HEALTH CENTER

****

Claire and Andrew walk through a sterile, clinical hallway at Corrigan Mental Health Center, their shoes squeaking along the freshly polished floor.

"So, um, how's Molly?" he asks.

"She'll come around," Claire tells him. "Just give her time."

They stop at a closed door. Claire puts an arm around the timid teenager and gives a motherly squeeze. "Everybody needs time to get settled and adjust to things, you know? You good?"

Andrew is reluctant, but Claire nods for him to enter – he needs to do this alone. After some hesitation, he gathers up courage then steps inside, unaware of what to expect.

At the far end of the room is James Wilden sitting in a chair by the window looking overwhelmed and distant.

Andrew slowly walks towards his father.

"Hey, Dad. How...how you doin'?" he asks timidly.

Mr. Wilden's face is a mixture of joy and sadness at the sight of his son. Andrew can tell his father is embarrassed by the surroundings and situation.

Andrew speaks first. "I'm sorry I haven't come by. I wanted to, but they said you needed some time..."

His father interrupts. "Your eye," he says tenderly touching the bruise on his son's face "What happened to your eye?"

"Nothing. I'm fine," Andrew reassures him. "Just, some kids at school."

Mr. Wilden raises an eyebrow. "School? You're in school?"

After a moment, he replies, "That's good."

The squeak of shoes is heard outside the hallway as a kind Nurse approaches. "How are we doing today, Mr. Wilden? This must be your son. So handsome."

Andrew looks around the room. "Could you bring my dad a television? He likes to watch movies."

"We thought it was best to keep him busy with other activities," the Nurse tells him. "Your father has a very full schedule."

"Oh. OK," Andrew replies, then turns to his father. "Dad, I need to tell you something. I, um. I saw m..."

What Andrew wants to say is, 'Mom. I saw Mom! She's back, here in Somerset, and we're all going to move home to the video store and live happily ever after, just like in the movies.' But he knows that's not the truth. He also knows that it's OK. It's all going to be OK.

Instead he says, "Movie. I saw a movie. It's about a kid who goes to a High School. He's the new kid, kind of a fish out of water, and..."

The *ding* of a text message is heard. The kind nurse reaches into the smock for her cell phone. "I'm sorry. I should have put that on mute."

"Get her. She's givin' out wings," smirks Mr. Wilden.

The nurse looks up. "Isn't that from IT'S A WONDERFUL LIFE? That's my favorite movie. Have you ever seen it?"

Mr. Wilden looks at Andrew and gives him a wink. *"Bing!"*

Andrew smiles wide.

"Now, son. You were telling me about this High School movie?" urges Mr. Wilden;

Andrew eagerly continues. "Yeah. Yeah. This kid has to go to a new school. He's the outcast, right? So, he needs to make all new friends and...."

Andrew continues to tell his father the story, and James Wilden's face lights up with every word.

FALL RIVER HIGH SCHOOL

****

Andrew walks the halls of his new school. This is clearly a different environment than Somerset High. It's tougher, more urban, dirty and crowded, but the kids are all the same. They hurry past, heads down on their cell phones, ignoring him, ignoring each other. They are all too busy texting, checking their Instagram posts, Facebook likes, and Snapchat stories.

Andrew stands alone at his locker struggling to get the combination open. It won't budge. Perfect. Here we go again.

Suddenly, a student rushes past.

"Dudes!" he yells to a crowd by the vending machines. "Did you hear what happened over at Somerset High? Check this out."

He holds up his cell phone to show the crowd a YouTube video. More kids gather to watch, all laughing and cheering as Skype's voice says, *"The question isn't who is going to let me; it's who is going to stop me."*

"This kids' got a hundred thousand likes already!" one person exclaims.

Andrew smiles, happy for his now Internet famous friend Skype.

O'HARA HOUSE

****

Andrew plops his backpack on the couch. It's been a long, miserable first day at the new school in Fall River. Pirates. Ugh.

The doorbell rings. Standing on Mrs. O'Hara's front porch is Molly holding cue cards in her hand. She puts a finger to her lips - Shhh! - re-enacting a scene from LOVE ACTUALLY.

She begins to drop the cards in succession:

...SOMETIMES...

...IT'S EASIER...

...TO BE OTHER PEOPLE...

A card shows pictures of Leonardo DiCaprio, Matthew Broderick, Emilio Esteves, Judd Nelson; all actors from the movies Andrew has quoted.

Molly continues to flip the cards.

...BUT, FOR FEAR OF COPYRIGHT ISSUES...

...AND BECAUSE I STILL DON'T OWN A TELEVISION...

...LET ME SAY...

...IN MY OWN WORDS...

...I LOVE YOU...

...ACTUALLY.

Andrew's eyes light up, "You saw that movie?!"

"Skype showed me. Have you seen it?" Molly asks innocently.   Andrew gives her a 'you're kidding me, right?' look.

"Some great lines in that movie," Molly adds with a smirk.

"There are," Andrew admits. "But I think it's time I start using my own words."

Molly smiles.

"Besides," he says stepping in close, "not *everything* I need is in the movies."

He wraps an arm around Molly's waist, pulls her body close and they kiss.

CHILD PROTECTIVE SERVICES OFFICE

****

'This is it,' Claire thinks to herself, staring at her mess of an office. 'Today is the day. Today I start to arrange things. Organize things. Toss things out. Get my life together.'

She leans back and scans the disheveled office one more time, and sighs, "Maybe tomorrow."

Claire looks out the window and sees a police car parked outside the building. Thinking (*hoping*) it's Danny Muldoon, she leaps out of the chair.

"Miss Peterson?" says Officer Kobolowski approaching her office. Claire can't mask her disappointment.

"Yes? Oh my God, what's wrong. Is it Ben? My mother?"

"No, no. Everyone is fine," Kobolowski reassures her. "I promise. But you'll need to come with me."

"Why?" asks Claire full of suspicion.

Kobolowski puffs his chest – he loves this part of the job. "Police business, Ma'am. If you could come with me, please?"

****

213

The police squad car pulls up to Danny Muldoon's complex. Claire gets out, totally confused.

"Go ahead," Kobolowski urges her, then rolls his eyes and mumbles, "Communication is *so* over-rated."

Before Claire can knock, the door swings open. She steps into Muldoon's apartment and looks around in awe. The whole place has been completely and magically transformed to look like an Italian restaurant. A red and white checkered table cloth covers a table set for two. Wine bottles drip wax from lit candles. Colorful posters of Rome, Venice and Florence cover the walls.

Music begins to play: *"'Oh this is the night, such a beautiful night, and they call it bella notte'"*

Muldoon steps out from the kitchen as if he just walked off a GQ magazine shoot. Two-piece tailored suit. Fitted shirt. Crisp tie. His hair coiffed with just the right amount of gel. He is handsome as hell. Claire swoons with delight.

"I did some recon on the flowers this time," he says walking towards her. Then, from behind his back, he hands her a huge bouquet -- of tulips. "I figured, who needs Italy? This is good right? Right?"

Claire throws her hands to her mouth in a gasp of pure delight. She wipes away a tear and collects herself. "Danny, you know I wanted to let Andrew stay, but..."

He presses a finger to her lips, "Talking is so over rated," then pulls Claire close and kisses her firmly, passionately.

Right on cue, Skype's head *pops* between them to ruin the moment. He's dressed like a waiter in a black suit, thin tie, black mustache, and butchers an Italian accent.

"'Here-a you are. The best-a spaghetti and meat-a ball in-a town.'"

Skype escorts Claire and Muldoon to the romantic table set for two, then stands at attention with a white towel draped over his arm awaiting their order. He glances down at Muldoon and motions with his eyes, as if urging him, "Go on. Go on. Do it!"

Muldoon leans down and begins to push a meatball across the plate with his nose.

Claire looks at him with disgust. "Ewe, what? What are you doing?!"

Muldoon feels like an idiot. "Nothing," he says through gritted teeth. "I'm gonna kill that kid!"

"Tell her about my idea," says Skype returning with a bottle of wine. "Did you tell her about my idea?"

"No. Not yet," snaps Muldoon wiping the meatball sauce from his nose, still angry at himself for ever listening to Skype's advice.

"Well, tell her!" demands Skype.

"God, you're annoying," Muldoon grumbles.

Skype abruptly stops pouring the wine. "Woah, woah. Annoying? Like, I'm the 'annoying sidekick?' I don't think so, dude. I'm more like the cool shadow character. Or the seasoned mentor who helps the hero's journey."

"You are not the mentor," Muldoon tells him flatly.

"Sure, I am," says Skype.

"Not even close."

"Yes. I am."

Claire intervenes. "   Guys. Guys! The idea?"

****

Andrew and Claire sit in the front seat of her car, face to face, eye to eye. There is a seriousness in the air as they each take a deep breath.

"You sure about this?" asks Andrew.

"Never been surer of anything in my life," says an overly confident Claire.

"I don't know," replies a reluctant Andrew.

"Listen to me," Claire tells him. "You're gonna be OK. I promise." She pauses, then says, "This is good, right?"

Andrew smiles back. "Right."

Suddenly Skype's head *pops* up beside the passenger window.

"Yo!" he shouts. "Wait till you see the new TV we put in my brother's room. Panasonic 65 inch Ultra Hi Def Premium. Firefox compatible. Dolby audio 2.0, high grade HDR playback. Dude, it's sweet!" He reaches in for Andrew's duffle bag then takes off.

"He seems pretty excited," Claire says to Andrew.

"Yeah. But I think I'm gonna lay off TV for a while. Maybe read a book. Molly tells me they're actually better than movies. Can you believe that?" he says dripping with sarcasm.

Claire nods with a smirk, "I've heard that, yes."

She clicks a colored pen and opens a unicorn notebook.

"Alright. Proper forms are all in order," she says with confidence.

"Look at you," says Andrew with a smile. "So organized. Do me a favor and check in on Muldoon for me, will ya? Make sure he's not watching too much television."

"Roger that," says Claire, mocking her boyfriend.

Andrew hops out, closes the car door, then leans back in through the open window.

"And you," he says to someone in the back seat. "Make sure someone shows you around that new school. Like, where the cool kids sit and stuff. You're gonna want the right crew."

Ben sits buckled in the back. Name tag. Lunch box. Hair slicked.

"'*So long... partner,*'" he replies, ready for school.

Claire looks up at the Johnson family, all waiting for Andrew by their front door. She turns to Andrew and says, "'*I think this is the beginning of a beautiful friendship.*'"

"Hey! I thought you didn't watch movies!" Andrew exclaims.

Claire just smiles and shrugs, then watches Andrew bounce up the stairs to his new home.

Happy.

Confident.

He belongs.

ANDREW'S MOVIE LINES:

In order of appearance

"Get her. She's givin' out wings" - **It's A Wonderful Life**

"Good morning, dear. And in case I don't see ya, good afternoon, good evening, and good night!" - **The Truman Show**

"Don't mess with the bull, young man. You'll get the horns."

- **The Breakfast Club**

"Bing!" - **Groundhog Day**

"Okay, campers, rise and shine, and don't forget your booties 'cause it's cooooold out there today. It's coooold out there every day." - **Groundhog Day**

"You come on down here and chum some of this sh..." - **Jaws**

"Saddle up. We're burning daylight!" - **The Cowboys**

"Come on, Dad. Dad. Dad. Dad, Dad, Dad." - **Lion King**

"Eat. My. Shorts." - ***The* Breakfast Club**

"The athlete. The basketcase. The princess. The criminal." - **The Breakfast Club**

"Hasta la Vista, baby." - **The Terminator**

"You're gonna need a bigger boat" - **Jaws**

"Yes, I got a question. Does Barry Manilow know you raid his wardrobe?" - **The Breakfast Club**

"See this? This is this. This ain't something else. This is this."

 - **The Deerhunter**

"You got any white bread?" - **The Blues Brothers**

"I'll have some toasted white bread, please." - **The Blues Brothers**

"We're on a mission from God." - **The Blues Brothers**

"Shall we play a game?" - **War Games**

"You want jam on that dry white toast, Honey?" - **The Blues Brothers**

"Just you and me. Two hits. Me hitting you. You hitting the floor." - **The Breakfast Club**

"Leave the gun. Take the cannoli." - **The Godfather**

"*Arise, fair sun, and kill the envious moon, That thou, her maid, art far more fair than she.*"   - **Romeo and Juliet**

"*I was just gonna say - four o'clock*". - **Ghostbusters**

"*You're my density*" - **Back to the Future**

"*We're all pretty bizarre. Some of us are just better at hiding it, that's all.*" **The Breakfast Club**

"*You know, it's legal for me to take you down to the station and sweat it out of you under the lights.*" -***Dick Tracy***

"*Juuuust a bit outside.*" - **Major League**

"*You're killing me, Smalls. You're killing me!*" - **The Sandlot**

"*Pick me out a winner, Bobby.*" **– The Natural**

"There's no crying in baseball!" - **A League of Their Own**

"Hey batta hey batta batta batta SWING batta!"

- Ferris Beuller's Day Off

"Serve the public, protect the innocent, uphold the law."

 - RoboCop

"Waiter, there is too much pepper on my paprikash." "But I would be proud to partake of your pecan pie." - **When Harry Met Sally**

"There is no try. Only Do." - **Return of the Jedi**

"Would you like to go to the movies with me tonight?" - **When Harry Met Sally**

"Eat me." - **Animal House**

"You gonna bark all day little doggie...or are you gonna bite?"- **Reservoir Dogs**

"Hey bud, what's your problem?" - **Fast Times at Ridgemont High**

"You are a sad strange little man. And you have my pity." - **Toy Story**

"Frankly, my dear, I don't give a damn." - **Gone With The Wind**

"I'm so cold Jack." - **Titanic**

"Hold on tight spider monkey." - **Twilight**

"Nobody puts baby in a corner." - **Dirty Dancing**

"There's a new Sherriff in town. Ya'll be cool." - **48 Hours**

"You can be my wing man anytime." - **Top Gun**

"Just keep swimming." - **Finding Nemo**

"To infinity and beyond!" - **Toy Story**

"Aaaarrrrrggghh ---Kelly Clarkson!" - **40 Year Old Virgin**

"Grab a drink, don't cost nothin'." - **Animal House**

"Bring me a pitcher of beer every seven minutes until somebody passes out. Then bring one every 10 minutes." **- Back to School**

"We're goin' streakin' in the quad!" **- Old School**

"I am a Golden God!" **- Almost Famous**

"The first rule of Fight Club is: You do not talk about Fight Club." **- Fight Club**

"Say 'what' again. I dare you. I double dare you." **- Pulp Fiction**

"If done right...can no defense." **- Karate Kid**

"There are a lot of things about me you don't know anything about. Things you wouldn't understand. Things you couldn't understand. Things you shouldn't understand." **- Pee Wee's Big Adventure**

"Mother? Mother, where are you?" **- Bambi**

"I have a feeling we're not in Kansas anymore." **- Wizard of Oz**

"We are fighting for our right to live. To exist. "We will not go quietly into the night!" We will not vanish without a fight! We're going to live on! We're going to survive! Today we celebrate our Independence Day!" **- Independence Day**

"Would you be willin' to trade ALL the days, for one chance, just one chance, to tell our enemies that they may take our homework...but they'll never take...OUR FREEDOM!"

- Braveheart

"Oh this is the night, such a beautiful night, and they call it bella notte" **- Lady and the Tramp**

"Here-a you are. The best-a spaghetti and meat-a ball in-a town." **- Lady and the Tramp**

"So long, Partner." **– Toy Story 3**

"I think this is the beginning of a beautiful friendship."

– Casablanca

This story was inspired by documentaries:

THE WOLF PACK - A coming of age story following the six Angulo brothers who have spent their entire lives locked away from society in an apartment on the Lower East Side of Manhattan. All they know of the outside world is gleaned from the films they watch obsessively and recreate meticulously, using elaborate homemade props and costumes. For years this has served as a productive way to stave off loneliness — but when one of the brothers escapes, everything changes.

LIFE, ANIMATED - the inspirational story of Owen Suskind, a young man who was unable to speak as a child until he and his family discovered a unique way to communicate by immersing themselves in the world of classic Disney animated films.

Also by Mike Bernard

CROSSING GUARDS

Megan Hayes is a hospice nurse from the blue-collar streets of South Boston. Haunted by the memory of her mother dying in an empty house, Megan vows to never let a patient die alone. But with her Irish temper and bad dating record, Megan fears that she may never find love, and will ultimately end up alone herself.

Living with her father doesn't help. Jackie Boy Hayes is a 68 year old, fitness-crazed former US Marine. Check that - no such thing as a former Marine. He IS a Marine! Jackie Boy spends his days seeking new and interesting ways to exercise, and finds an unlikely new recruit in a lonesome, overweight teenager. When Megan falls for a patient's married son, she will uncover shocking revelations and learn that there is more to life than waiting for it to end.

CROSSING GUARDS is an uplifting story about finding love and friendship in unlikely places, reminding us to keep our hearts open and soldier on. Semper Fi

Available on Amazon.com

A FISHERMAN'S VIEW

After their mother's death, colorful Irish patriarch Michaleen Fitzgerald gives his estranged children three plastic baggies – RED, GREEN, YELLOW - to scatter her ashes at specific locations. The symbolism is not lost on them. Theresa is the angry one, Richard is materialistic, and Fiona is crippled with anxieties. But they're wrong. The colors represent something else entirely, and the journey to dispose the ashes and find their true meanings and destinations has just begun.

With dark but tender humor, Michaleen helps his children take a different view of life, hoping they'll grab it by the lapels and swing it back onto the dance floor, but each child is harboring complicated feelings and secrets that threaten to tear their family apart.

A FISHERMAN'S VIEW is a deeply emotional story of reconciliation and a celebration of family; how people who were raised so close can be so far apart without truly knowing it.

Available on Amazon.com

ABOUT THE AUTHOR

Mike Bernard is a founding partner of The ChathamPoint Group, an executive search firm outside Boston, MA. His 'midlife crisis' writing career began when his children and his money went off to college - checks made out to Loyola University Maryland (x2) and Assumption College respectively. Mike's work has placed in the NICHOLL FELLOWSHIP, BLUECAT, and FINAL DRAFT Big Break Screenplay contests, and was a TOP 10 FINALIST in the PAGE International screenplay competition. Three of his screenplays were optioned and under development with production companies.

Mike is a graduate of Providence College and Boston College High School. He resides in Medfield, MA with his wife Michele.

He spends summers on the beaches of Cape Cod and winters roaming the aisles of Home Depot.

Contact: Meb123@comcast.net

Made in the USA
Middletown, DE
20 July 2019